BEANY MALONE

BEANY
MALONE

LENORA MATTINGLY WEBER

Thomas Y. Crowell Company
New York

BY THE AUTHOR

Meet the Malones
Beany Malone
Leave It to Beany!
Beany and the Beckoning Road
My True Love Waits
Beany Has a Secret Life
Make a Wish for Me
Happy Birthday, Dear Beany
The More the Merrier
A Bright Star Falls
Welcome, Stranger
Pick a New Dream
Tarry Awhile
Something Borrowed, Something Blue
Come Back, Wherever You Are
The Beany Malone Cookbook
Don't Call Me Katie Rose
The Winds of March
A New and Different Summer
I Met a Boy I Used to Know

COPYRIGHT 1948 BY LENORA MATTINGLY WEBER

Published in Canada by Fitzhenry & Whiteside Limited, Toronto

MANUFACTURED IN THE UNITED STATES OF AMERICA

ISBN 0-690-12455-4

18   19   20   21

TO
KATHLEEN LENORA WEBER

I

Cape-and-Sword Norbett

This windy Saturday in October had started with such a gusty happiness. But then all Saturdays in the big Malone home were a hectic, happy hullabaloo with young folks coming and going, with bath water running, with someone standing at the top of the stairs yelling to someone in the kitchen, with the telephone in the back hall ringing—forever ringing.

Sixteen-year-old Catherine Cecilia Malone—known as Beany to family and friends—had started the day with nothing more weighty on her mind than whether they should make chocolate or peppermint-stick ice cream for the party she was putting on this afternoon (and whether the freckle cream she was secretly buying at the drugstore would dim the marching formation of freckles across her nose). She had no idea that she would be a different Beany by the time the day ended. She had no idea that the Malone way which had seemed so *right* that morning would seem so *wrong* by nightfall.

1

Beany was in the kitchen now, making seven-minute icing for the cake her older brother Johnny was watching in the oven. The cake had been delayed by Johnny's frequent dashes to the telephone. On the kitchen table, the drainboards, even the stove's top, was the floury, spilled-sugar, egg-shell clutter that always accompanied this creative feat of Johnny's.

The sprinkling of freckles across Beany's nose was almost lost in the warm flush of her square-chinned face as she vigorously whipped the icing in the double boiler. Her stubby brown braids, which she wore pinned up now that she was a high-school sophomore, kept jiggly time to the egg beater. "They ought to call this seven*teen*-minute icing," she grumbled with her eye on the clock, which said five after one; and the party was to be at two.

At first Johnny's Lady Eleanor cake had soared to such beautiful heights. "Look at that," Johnny bragged with the oven door open a crack. "It takes creative genius to make a cake like that. Light as a snowflake in spring."

"It takes fifteen egg whites," Beany reminded him practically.

But on the next peek Lady Eleanor wasn't doing so well. She was falling in the middle, and about that Johnny waxed philosophical. "Just like life. Your hopes lift so high and then somehow there comes a sag. . . . Beany, do you suppose you could fill in that depression with icing?"

"Oh, sure," Beany said.

Johnny pulled out a broom straw to test it. Johnny was eighteen. He was tall and thin, with a light-footed grace and a shock of curly black hair. Beany, the most practical of all the Malones, was always scolding him about not getting his hair cut. To which Johnny always retorted,

"Beany, my pigeon, a genius is supposed to be long-haired."

But it was Johnny's smile that set him apart from his fellow men. It wasn't only that it revealed such a perfect set of teeth that the Malone dentist said once he'd like to hire Johnny to sit in his waiting room and smile. His smile had that rare and heart-warming quality of making you one with his plans; it was appealing and gently apologetic. At Harkness High, where Beany was a sophomore and Johnny a senior, other students said it was Johnny's smile, as much as his ability for writing, that melted the grumpiest teacher.

Even Mrs. No-complaint Adams, who gave the Malones the last half of every day to "wash, iron, and cook them," was never grim about ten minutes extra if she was ironing Johnny's sport shirts. But then Mrs. Adams was partial to the menfolks in the motherless Malone household. Little Martie she referred to fondly as "the little mister." And as for Martie Malone, father of the Malones! Mrs. Adams was sure that if the president at Washington would just read Martie Malone's editorials in the *Morning Call*, he would be entirely fit to cope with all the world's problems.

This Saturday noon Mrs. Adams' iron thumped rhythmically in what the family called the butler's pantry though, as Johnny said, no butler had ever sanctified it by his presence. They called their housekeeper Mrs. No-complaint Adams because it was her proud boast that she had "worked out" for seventeen years and had never had a complaint. The next-door neighbor to the south was also a Mrs. Adams. The Malones differentiated by calling her Mrs. Socially-prominent Adams. The society page never missed mentioning one of her teas, luncheons, or committee meetings.

Out on the back porch Elizabeth, Beany's oldest sister,

was turning the ice-cream freezer. She came in, her hands
clammy and cold from working with ice and salt. "Beany,
see if it turns hard enough to take out the dasher. Oh,
Beany, warm my hands." Beany chafed them between her
warm ones. . . . Oh Elizabeth, Beany thought, I wish I
could warm your heart that's so empty and waiting for word
from Don. . . .

Elizabeth Malone McCallin was a war bride. It was her
three-year-old Martie—the little mister—who was hanging
on to Johnny's leg as he reached to a high cupboard shelf
for the glass cake plate. Little Martie's hair was three
shades lighter than his mother's, and curled about his face
like an angel's on a Christmas card. Ever so often the Malone family would gird themselves to get those curls cut off.
After all, they didn't want to make a sissy out of him! Once
Johnny had even got him as far as Charlie's barber shop
on the boulevard. But Johnny brought him back, his fair
fluff of curls intact. "Charlie, himself, wasn't there," Johnny
excused. "And little Martie and I didn't vibrate to those
slap-dash helpers."

Before Elizabeth married she had gone a year to the
university. She had been strenuously rushed by every sorority and pledged by the "prominent" Delts. She had been
chosen freshman escort for the Homecoming queen. And,
before the year was out, she had been married under
crossed swords to Lieutenant Donald McCallin. But now
the war was over. Soldiers were returning. But Elizabeth
was still waiting for Don to return from overseas.

Elizabeth was lovable and loving—and so lovely! Oh,
why couldn't I, Beany often thought, have hair that makes
a shining aureole about my face (as they say in books)? Why

couldn't boys send me violets and say they were pale compared to my eyes? "Beany is so capable," everyone said. . . .
But doggonit, when you were a high-school sophomore and
your heart's eyes always followed one certain boy down the
hall, it wasn't enough to be tagged as capable. . . .

Johnny found the box with the dozen pink candles and
the fullblown rose candle holders. "Good thing Jock isn't
thirteen," he said, laying them on the table.

"He's twelve," Beany said, "and he never had a birthday
party."

"He'll be here any minute," Johnny said. "Him and
Lorna. Bet they've had Miss Hewlitt up since the break of
day."

"I know," Beany laughed, and her spirits lifted. What
was more fun than all this making ice cream and cake for
a little boy, shunted for safekeeping out of his own country
to a rheumatic old uncle Charley? A little boy, who had
never had a birthday party and who had been counting the
days until this first Saturday in October.

Jock and Lorna were two English children who had been
sent over to a great-uncle when England's bombing threatened their safety. The great-uncle was the gardener and
handy man for Miss Hewlitt, English Lit teacher at Harkness High and long-time friend of the Malones. In their
young loneliness Jock and Lorna had made the Malone
home their second home—their preferred home. Never a
weekend passed without Jock tagging garrulously after
Beany, without Lorna bobbing in and out of the house,
paying court with carrots and lettuce leaves to Beany's big
white rabbit, Frank. Beany had got in the habit of saving
every piece of ribbon to tie on Lorna's hair. Great-uncle

Charley or the busy Miss Hewlitt thought a rubber band or piece of string was sufficient to hold a little girl's hair in place.

So Beany vigorously beat the icing until it "formed a peak," visualizing as she did Jock's happy swagger when he saw the cake. Beany's capable fingers slivered off the high part on Johnny's cake and filled in the sunken spot. She slid a newspaper under the cake plate to catch any dripping icing. It was the *Morning Call* for which her father wrote editorials.

As she iced the cake her eyes noted that the paper was open at one of his sizzling editorials about unfit cars, careless drivers, and the mounting rate of traffic injuries and fatalities. Her knife scooped up a dab of icing off a line that read, "When is our safety manager, N. J. Rhodes, going to waken from his long nap and do something about this?"

Beany knew an unhappy squirming. It was the irony of fate that her crusading father should be nipping at the heels of the lax N. J. Rhodes while Beany was secretly ordering freckle cream for the benefit of his nephew, Norbett Rhodes, who sat next to her in typing. All other classes at Harkness were just classes—but fifth hour her typewriter was next to the one on which Norbett's restless fingers pounded. "What is it two of in *occasion*—two *c*'s or two *s*'s?" he had asked her. Oh, thank goodness, she could spell! Maybe he hadn't noticed the freckles, or her hair, which Beany, in her pessimistic moments, called "roan." Just yesterday he had asked her, "How would you write the possessive of Haas?"

There, the cake was beautifully iced.

Beany reached for the candle holders and discovered a minor tragedy. Little Martie had chewed on four—no, five—of the rose holders until they resembled worm-eaten rosebuds.

It was always surprising that anyone with as beatific an expression as Little Martie's could get in as much trouble as he did. It was always surprising, too, when little Martie spoke. He didn't talk a baby-talk jumble, but with a slow, feeling-his-way accuracy. "I—like—these," he said slowly, reproachfully, when Beany pried the demolished roses out of his fingers.

Johnny offered to run up to Downey's drugstore for more, but Beany said firmly, "Not you. I'll go." As though Johnny could buy a *few* candle holders. He'd come back with five dozen. Wasn't Beany still using the pint bottle of almond extract he had bought over three years ago when a recipe had called for a few drops of almond extract?

Beany grabbed Johnny's khaki jacket from the back of a chair and started down the back steps for the drugstore, five blocks away. If the freckle cream was there she'd pick it up, too.

She entered the drugstore breathlessly, with her mind entirely on the candle holders, and hoping that if the icing dripped Johnny would knife it up and put it back onto the cake. Then her heart did a hollow hop, skip, and jump. Norbett Rhodes was standing at the magazine rack, thumbing through a magazine.

Instinctively Beany's two hands reached out and caught her short flappy braids under her combs. Oh, why did she have to meet Norbett Rhodes, wearing this messy plaid seersucker under Johnny's faded, shapeless jacket!

Norbett said, "Hi, Beany!" and she said, "Hi, Norbett!" and stood so he wouldn't see the dab of icing on her skirt.

But the fountain mirror, with its pasted-on patches telling of sundaes and sandwiches, showed a girl with cheeks
as pink as the peppermint-stick ice cream that she had mixed
earlier. Her eyes weren't the violet blue of Elizabeth's, but
a gray-blue shadowed by short but very thick eyelashes. Her
"roan" hair hadn't the golden high lights of Elizabeth's, but
it had a soap-and-water, a well-brushed shine. Beany's prettiness was of the honest, hardy variety.

The druggist, behind the fountain, called out, "Beany,
the freckle cream I ordered for you came. Want to take it?"

"No—no—" she faltered. "I just want some pink candle
holders." If only Norbett was too preoccupied with his
magazine to notice.

Last year, when Norbett Rhodes was a senior and Beany
was in Junior High, she had gone to the Harkness Spring
Opera in which Norbett sang the lead. A Viking prince in
blue velvet cape with a scarlet lining and a clanking sword,
always ready to loose the shackles of the oppressed. Beany,
in Harkness parlance, had "fallen on her face" for the
senior with his reddish hair, his intense hazel eyes, his stirring Nelson Eddy voice.

She always saw him as cape-and-sword Norbett, even when
he sat hunched over his typewriter until Miss Meigs, their
typing teacher, reminded him, "Watch your posture, Norbett." And yet her dream of being Norbett's girl was so
hopelessly gummed up. For Beany was realist enough to
know that Norbett liked her sister, Mary Fred, and yet
disliked Mary Fred because she wouldn't date him. And,
even worse, she, Beany, was Martie Malone's daughter. And
Martie Malone was viciously berating Norbett's uncle—
N. J. Rhodes, safety manager—for his indifferent enforce-
ment of traffic laws. It was this uncle and his wife with

whom Norbett made his home at the big Park Gate Hotel.

Norbett was still at Harkness High and was vindictively bitter and resentful about being there. Norbett's enemies—and unlike Johnny he had a goodly number—said he had been so busy being a big shot his senior year that he had overshot himself and failed to graduate. Norbett was school reporter for the *Tribune*, rival paper of Martie Malone's *Call*. During the winter, when he had covered a ski meet and had been overanxious for a good picture shot, he had climbed a high ledge and slipped and torn a ligament in his ankle. He had missed many chemistry classes because the chem lab was on third floor.

But even so, Norbett was a good enough student, so that all the school was startled when the chemistry professor announced two days before graduation that he was failing Norbett Rhodes. Old stand-pat Professor Bagley! Old Baggy, the students said, thought no boy or girl was equipped to enter the wider realm of life until he or she had mastered the "Nitrogen Cycle."

Norbett opened the heavy drugstore door for Beany, held it against the dusty wind, which promptly ballooned out Beany's jacket and tugged at her braids. "How about a lift home?" he asked. "My wagon's got a new paint job. Shade your eyes when you look at it."

The new paint job was as brightly red as Superman's famous cloak as front-paged on the comic books in the store. "Almost hides all the dents in the fenders," Norbett said, as he swung behind the wheel beside Beany. He asked too casually, "What's Mary Fred doing today?"

"She's going to a Delt tea," Beany said. She thought wretchedly, he's just taking me home, hoping he'll see Mary Fred—or at least show off the new paint job on his car.

("Old show-off Norbett," Mary Fred always said. "Old hot-stuff himself!")

In the drugstore Norbett had been just a moody, studious, too-thin boy of eighteen or nineteen in a loud sport jacket. But in his red flash of car he took on a reckless, man-about-town swagger. He shot out from the curb. He jabbed a perilous fender-grazing course through the traffic headed for the football game.

"Be careful, Norbett," Beany cried out once, as he barely missed an elderly woman, carrying two bulging sacks of groceries.

"Pedestrians have eyes and legs," he said. "What's to hinder them from being careful?"

"Old people and children can't," she argued.

"Listen at her! Martie Malone's daughter. Brake-and-light Malone, we call him. Impound-the-cars Malone! Him, and his screaming editorials. All the young folks in town would like to strangle him. Old Killjoy Malone! He's slowed traffic on the Boulevard here to twenty-five an hour. What does he want—a funeral procession?"

Beany defended, "He wants to cut down accidents."

Norbett swung onto Barberry street. The white-pillared colonial home of Mrs. Socially-prominent Adams occupied a spacious corner. Its snow-white pillars made its red brick even redder. It had a starched and preening dressiness with its shutters, its ruffled curtains looped back from every window, its window-boxes, brightly splotched now with purple asters. Like a woman dressed for a party in necklace, earrings—even a corsage.

On the far corner was the dark-brick, unadorned home of Judge Buell. Its solid front and massive door had a grim, dignified, even judicial façade. Even the ivy, now a copper red, climbed with watchful decorum up the side. The hedge was squarely trimmed in a "thus far and no farther shalt thou go" manner.

In between sat the wide-bosomed, gray stone Malone home, with its winding driveway at the side. Sitting between these two carefully planned, well-tended homes, the Malone home had neither a starched preeningness nor a grim dignity but rather a scuffed, "come in as you are" friendliness. The Malone barberry hedge, given its own way, was bright with red berries. Their ivy had reached the windows in Father's room and spread protectingly across them.

The mother of the Malones had been the enthusiastic gardener of the family, and though she had been dead five years now, each spring brought glad and surprising remembrances of her. A few little crocuses pushing up in an unexpected corner; a flowering almond bursting into pink glory where they thought bridal wreath held sway. "Mary must have set that out," Father would say. And each time it was like an extra warm smile from her.

Folks driving to the Malone home always whirled into the driveway, for the Malone entrance was on the side, the steps flanked by two sentinel conifer trees. But Norbett Rhodes, as though the Malone driveway was too intimate for a Rhodes, stopped in the street outside with a screech and scream of brakes.

"Well, well," he mocked. "Only two children in the Malone yard!"

"Oh, Jock and Lorna are here already! And the candles aren't on the cake yet!"

"Your place used to look like an orphan asylum when I'd drive past."

Beany said flatly, "Those were the three Biddinger children. Their parents were killed at Pearl Harbor and so Father sent them home to us. They lived with us two years and then—then their uncle down in Santa Fe took them. Marcella—she was just ten when she came—" Beany's flushed face clouded, her voice choked, "I—missed Marcella—so. Our house seemed so—empty after they left."

Norbett's eyes flicked over the woe in her face. He said, "You Malones certainly stick your neck out for trouble. Didn't you know those orphans from Hawaii wouldn't be with you for keeps? You're a funny kid, Beany. You're so doggoned honest. But you care too much about things. Don't you know there's no percentage in that?"

Beany said impulsively, "Look, Norbett, we've got peppermint-stick ice cream and a birthday cake. I wish you'd come to the party."

He looked at her mockingly. "Don't you know I'm the Malone enemy? All up and down the line. Your father is out tooth and nail after my uncle Norbett. Your sister Mary Fred told me once I had a mean disposition—she said I ought to eat more carrots. And Johnny—well, your genius Johnny and I have always locked horns."

"You mean about all those prize essays and class plays at school?"

"I've never once got the best of Johnny Malone. Last year when I was a senior and he was a junior he always outsmarted me. And this year I've got a swell idea for a senior play, but I suppose if Johnny Malone gets up with some half-baked idea of his, he'll have them all eating out of his hand. I lie awake at night, dreaming of the time when I'll have revenge on the Malones. Shakespeare said a mouthful when he said,

If I can catch him once upon the hip
I will feed fat the ancient grudge I bear him.

Oh yes, and another thing. If you think my uncle Norbett is easy to live with since Martie Malone started nipping at his heels, you're crazy."

What could Beany say? She was torn between loyalty for the Malones and her own secret longing to reach out to him and say, "I'm not your enemy, Norbett."

Norbett said, "I'm covering the football game for the *Tribune* this aft. How about you dashing out there with me? We can get in on my Press pass. I might need you on the spelling."

Beany's heart lifted high under Johnny's faded jacket. He was asking *her*. He wasn't thinking of her as Mary Fred's sister. Mentally she was scurrying up the stairs and squirming into her red slipover sweater—and if Mary Fred hadn't worn her navy-blue Chesterfield with the sheepskin lining she'd wear it. Mentally she was feeling Norbett's hand under her elbow, guiding her through the crowded stadium. All the world would see that she was Norbett's girl.

Lorna came to the gate—a little nine-year-old girl with hair that needed Beany's fingers to straighten the part and anchor with a ribbon the curl that was blowing every which way. Lorna said wistfully, proddingly, "Jock says the candles burn on the cake and you blow at them."

Beany reached reluctantly for the car door. "Oh, I'd love to, Norbett, but I—we promised Jock a party. He's never had a party—or a birthday cake—"

"It won't take all afternoon, will it?" Norbett asked impatiently. "It isn't everybody I'd give a second chance to, but I'll telephone you between halves from the Press box.

You get this birthday fiddle-faddle off your hands and I'll run down from the stadium and pick you up. Okay?"

"Okay," Beany said.

His red car went careening down Barberry street.

Okay?—Beany questioned herself, tremulously and apprehensively. Just like playing with fire is okay.

2

Beany Locks Up Her Heart

Beany's fingers were shaky with excitement as she wedged the wispy little pink candles into the new candle holders. Norbett had asked her to go with him while he covered the high-school games! Now the party didn't seem so all-important. "Hurry up, Johnny, and dish up the ice cream," she called.

"I'll help," Elizabeth offered.

Her father drifted into the kitchen. Only part of Beany's mind heard him say, "Don't mind me, Beany, if I get in your way. I'm nervous as a cat. I'm waiting for an important phone call." Only part of Beany's mind noticed how loosely her father's tweed coat hung from his thin shoulders, and how deeply penciled were the tired lines in his face.

He halted once and watched Beany's fingers spacing the candles on the cake. "Johnny's masterpiece turned out pretty even this time?" he asked.

"One side fell—you know that oven!—but I covered it up," Beany said.

Mary Fred came down the stairs and through the back hall, her wooden shower-shoes clackety-clacking. She was in her white toweling robe and carrying her best navy-blue dress with its piqué collar and cuffs. "Beany," she asked nervously, "should I press this on the right or the wrong side?"

"Wrong," Beany said. "When are you going to the Delt tea?"

Mary Fred leaned against the kitchen doorframe and the very troubled desperation in her eyes came as a jolt to Beany. Mary Fred lowered her voice so that Martie Malone, who had drifted into the dining room, wouldn't hear. "I don't know whether I'm going or not, Beany. It depends on whether old Prof Bagley telephones me about my chem credits or not." Her heavy voice, so unlike Mary Fred's own buoyant voice, came as a jolt to Beany.

For the most notable thing about Mary Fred Malone was her exuberance, her sparkle, her "get-up-and-git," as Mrs. No-complaint Adams put it. Whenever Mary Fred came into a room she brought a quickening lift. Girls always said, "Mary Fred, you've *got* to come to the party. It's never so partyish without you."

Mary Fred wasn't as lovely as Elizabeth. Her hair missed that golden glint and was just a thick mop of curly brown hair. Her eyes weren't violet blue, but just blue eyes that twinkled with good humor, flashed with temper. Father always said about Mary Fred's and Beany's eyes, "It's an old Irish custom to put blue eyes in with a sooty finger and then shake the finger over the nose for a few freckles." (Only Mary Fred's freckles, Beany noticed, weren't as bold as hers.)

Mary Fred wasn't as capable, as soberly dependable, as Beany. She was impulsive and generous, vehement and loyal. "Old bubble-and-bounce Mary Fred," Johnny always called her.

Last March the father of the Malones had been on a plane that had had to make a crash landing on the Wyoming plains in a blizzard. None of the passengers had been hurt fatally, though many had been injured. Martie Malone, himself, had never mentioned his heroism, but other plane passengers had. They told about the first rescue truck coming through the snow to pick up the passengers, and Martie Malone insisting that he wasn't hurt and waiting hours for the truck to return for those remaining.

So that on top of broken ribs Martie Malone had a frightening case of pneumonia. The family had cared for him at home because the hospitals were full. Nor could they get full-time nurses. So it was Mary Fred who stayed home from school to take his temperature and watch over the oxygen tent. They had all helped, but Elizabeth had much ado to keep little Martie undisturbing and quiet. Johnny and Beany had been willing and anxious to help, but it was Mary Fred to whom the doctor gave detailed instructions. It was Mary Fred who, during his slow convalescence, hovered over him, feeding him broths, gruels, and custards. And it was Mary Fred who, when her class graduated, hadn't her chemistry notebook completed and couldn't receive her diploma. Even as Norbett Rhodes.

But this fall Mary Fred had enrolled at the university on condition that her chem credits be made up by the quarter's end. "One foot in heaven," Mary Fred put it, "and the other in that stinkin' lab at Harkness." For Mary Fred was being rushed by the Delts, Elizabeth's sorority. But the Delts would have to drop her like a hot potato unless she got her chem credits.

Mary Fred said, as she wet a finger and ticked it against the hot iron, "I begged old Baggy to telephone me and let me know—"

With that the telephone in the back hall pealed.

Whenever the telephone rang in the Malone home there was a sudden scurry. It was such an innocuous black instrument, sitting there on the shelf in the back hall, but on its silvery peal so much depended. Even Red, their dignified setter, always got in the way of the one hurrying to answer it; he had to be close at hand and know whether it was a happy call or a disappointing one.

Johnny's long legs were usually the swiftest at covering the distance. Today he quickly sidestepped little Martie, and straddled the dog, motioning as he went with the long ice-cream spoon in his hand, like a football player signaling that he would make the catch. He breathed out, as he passed Beany, "Oh golly, if this is only the landlady saying she's got hold of old Emerson Worth!"

Norbett's words leaped highlighted into Beany's mind. "You Malones certainly stick your neck out." Oh, why had Johnny stuck his neck out in helping old Emerson Worth write a book!

For three years Johnny had been working on Emerson's book manuscript, which was titled, *Our City Has Deep Roots.* "I am Emerson's amanuensis," Johnny said. "Meaning the pounder of the typewriter."

"Meaning," Beany had said, "the pounder on Emerson's back."

Emerson Worth was one of the builders of the city,

a once nationally known newspaperman. But, outliving his usefulness, he had been a bitter and defeated old man until Johnny had said, "Emerson, I'll help you write your book. Just spout to me and I'll put it on paper." Thus the book was begun. . . . An old man dreaming dreams and a young man seeing visions. . . . It had been Johnny's idea to hang the book together with items out of old newspapers and then to fill in with the story Emerson recounted. It was Johnny's dream that Emerson's dream be fulfilled.

But Beany, watching Johnny grab for the telephone, knew the fear that was haunting Johnny—the fear that Emerson would never be able to finish the book. For Emerson Worth, past his eightieth birthday, was often too vague and maundery to fill in the dates and facts that Johnny needed. This whole windy Saturday Johnny had been trying to get hold of him. Johnny felt responsible for him. Johnny was heartsick to think of the forgetful old fellow wandering the streets in the cold wind. "No telling when he's eaten last," Johnny had murmured today, as he had whipped egg whites.

I'm afraid for you, Johnny, Beany was thinking. I'm afraid you'll lose your race with time. For you know Dr. Hunter said Emerson's heart was like a leaky bicycle pump. Emerson has so many of these days when he promises to come out and work on his book with you—and then he forgets. But it's his book, it isn't yours, and you shouldn't care so hard about it. There's no percentage in that, as Norbett says.

The ringing telephone had brought Elizabeth rushing in from the ice-cream freezer on the back porch. Elizabeth, with leaping hope in her face. Elizabeth said her ears were getting pointed like a bird dog's, listening for that *certain* phone call. "Some day," she had said shakily to Beany, "I'll answer the phone and the operator will say, 'Long-distance calling Mrs. Donald McCallin.' And that will be Don!"

Oh, but Elizabeth, Beany worried, I wish you weren't waiting so hard. I wish your whole happiness didn't hang on a telephone call.

Beany could see her father in the dining room. He had been putting chairs up to the table, but now he stood, waiting, hoping to hear the words, "For you, Dad!"

Martie Malone was waiting for a telephone call to tell him the outcome of the city council's meeting. To tell him whether or not it had passed a law to impound the cars of all traffic violators. But it shouldn't matter so much to you whether they pass it or not, Beany thought. You should have gone away as Dr. Hunter told you and rested and got strong after your pneumonia, instead of staying here all summer and fall, working so hard on your crusade. You look so thin and tired. Why should you go on sticking your neck out and worrying about mounting traffic accidents?

At the telephone's first ring Mary Fred had dropped the iron with a clop on its stand and started a clackety-clack trek toward the telephone. But Johnny was ahead of her. There was no bubble, no bounce to Mary Fred now. Just a tense hope that the voice on the telephone would be Professor Bagley from Harkness High telling her that her make-up chem experiments were passing.

Oh, Mary Fred, Beany ached for her, I can't bear for that old ghoul of a Baggy to keep you on tenterhooks like this. If only Father hadn't thought of the others on the plane and had thought first of Martie Malone! Then you'd have graduated with your class. You'd be wearing your Delt pledge pin by now. You'd be tearing around getting ready for the Delt tea.

"Hello," Johnny yelled into the telephone. "This is Johnny—"

"Can't you say, 'The Malone Residence'?" Mary Fred prodded nervously. "Not 'This is Johnny,' like a Philip Morris radio program."

Johnny turned disappointedly from the telephone. "It's your little pal Lila, Mary Fred, all a-tizzy about what you're going to wear to the tea—and what time shall she stop for you?"

Elizabeth went dispiritedly back to the dishing up of ice cream. Father began looking about for another chair to put up to the table.

Mary Fred said thinly, "Tell her I'm not going, Johnny."

"Aren't you going, Mary Fred?" Beany asked concernedly. "I'll press your dress for you."

Mary Fred shook her head. "Beany, I can't stand for all the Delts to ask me how I'm getting along in chem. They're so sort of polite about it, but I know what they're thinking. No chem credit, no sorority. And, Beany, that cussed chem is just like a nightmare—a nightmare where you don't wake up."

Jock's birthday party got under way with a noisy swing. Only little Martie, his pale curls damp from a recent comb, sat in his high chair, so awed and excited he was momentarily quiet. So was the toy ocarina momentarily quiet. Johnny and Beany had bought it for Jock and it had come complete with playing instructions for "Home Sweet Home" and "Alexander's Ragtime Band." All the time the chairs were being put up to the table and the ice cream piled into glass sauce dishes, Jock had filled the house with weird notes. "We shall have music," Johnny said.

Jock's pleased swagger was satisfying payment for all their effort. Stocky young Jock with his cockney accent— he pronounced "say" as "s'y." He had a paternal bossiness toward his sister, Lorna, who accepted his word as law.

Then came the grand climax when Beany carried in the birthday cake with the candles lighted, when they joined Johnny's hearty singing of, "Happy birthday to Jock. . . ."

Elizabeth had drawn the curtains to dim the dining room. "Make a wish," she prompted Jock, whose shining eyes were on the cake, "and if you blow out every candle on one blow, you'll get your wish."

Jock was just drawing a long breath, preparatory to a cyclonic gust, when the door knocker banged loudly.

"Hold everything!" Johnny ordered. "Maybe that's Emerson Worth. Maybe he came to and remembered the party after all."

Johnny came back to the dining room. With him was a man in corduroy pants and a soldier's fatigue jacket. Johnny announced puzzledly, "He's come to get Jock and Lorna. And he's in a big hurry."

They all sat there at the birthday table, with the candles flickering palely, and stared at the stranger as he explained. He was driving to New York to meet the boat from England which was bringing his English bride. And Jock's and Lorna's folks had written him—he drew out the letter— and asked him if he would pick up the children, take them with him to New York, and put them on the boat for England. Jock's and Lorna's father was home from the war now, and he was anxious for his family to be reunited.

Beany heard Elizabeth demur, "But you'll have to get their clothes."

He had already got all their luggage. It was loaded in his car. He had gone out to Miss Hewlitt's and she and their great-uncle Charley had packed all their belongings. They had tried to telephone the Malones to tell them the news, but the line was always busy. And he was in a hurry because he wanted to make it to the Kansas line tonight.

Jock's attention was pulled back by the fluttery light of the candles on the cake. Again he began assembling from his depths a mighty blowing breath. Then his ears caught the words, "We've got them passage on the *Queen Mary.* Lordee, it's big enough to hold a whole town."

"You s'y we're going on the *Queen Mary?*—did you hear that, Lorna? Is it bigger than the boat we came over on?"

"Lots bigger," the impatient caller said. "And we'd better be shoving off."

"Bigger, you s'y!" Jock shrieked. "Well, come on. Lorna, get your hat. Wait now, till I tie your sash. Now don't be slow."

It happened so swiftly. One minute they were all there at the table, intent on Jock blowing out the candles, waiting to hand him the cake knife to cut the cake. And then, in no time at all, the car was whisking out the driveway with Lorna and Jock bouncing on the back seat among the luggage.

Beany turned away from the front door. Her hand was lifted to wave—but neither Jock nor Lorna had turned to wave. That was the thing that hurt so. They were going in such a rush of excitement. If only Jock had said, "Wait till I blow out the candles on my cake." If only Lorna had said, "Beany, I'd like to take a piece of your cake with me." But the two had been all scampering chatter about going on the *Queen Mary,* about seeing the place in their garden at home where a bomb had blown out a hole, "bigger'n our hen house."

Beany walked slowly, deflatedly, back to the cluttered table where the pink wispy candles guttered low. Melted pink wax had run into the seven-minute icing. The pink ice cream was frothy pink lakes, threatening to overrun the fluted rims of the glass sauce dishes.

It took three listless breaths for Beany to blow out the candles. She moved laboredly, carefully—as though something inside of her were broken and the edges were grating together. It had hurt just like this when the Biddinger children left, she remembered desolately.

And then the dim, but long-gathering resentment and bitterness seethed through her hurt and emptiness. Wasn't I the fool to go sticking my neck out again, she berated herself. I should have learned from the Biddinger children's leaving that there's no percentage—except hurt—in getting so attached to somebody. I won't ever be such a fool again. From now on I'll keep my heart locked up.

Again the telephone rang. Again Johnny's long legs reached it first. Again Elizabeth, Mary Fred, and Father waited tautly—hoping—hoping. This time Johnny yelled, "Beany, it's Norbett Rhodes—for you."

She had to crowd down the leaping eagerness. Her arms twitched with longing to shove themselves into the red sweater and Mary Fred's Chesterfield with the black velvet collar. She was already feeling the cement steps her feet would be vaulting up with the bunched, cheering crowds impeding their progress. For Norbett would be just one step behind her, steadying her, pushing her a little . . .

But Beany reached out a determined arm and pulled that thoughtless, shining-eyed Beany back. Don't kid yourself, Beany Malone. Don't go sticking your neck out. Just remember it's Mary Fred that Norbett really likes. He's just asking you to be asking somebody, maybe hoping he can make Mary Fred jealous. (Which, of course, he can't because Mary Fred has her own near-steady at the university.) Don't forget that Norbett declared himself the Malone enemy; he's just waiting to "feed fat the ancient grudge." Look what happened to Juliet when she ran athwart the Capulet-Montague feud.

But Beany's square jaw was set in unhappy grimness. "Tell him I'm busy, Johnny. Tell—" she had to swallow twice, "tell him I'm sorry, but I'm too busy to go."

Busy gathering up dishes of sickish pink ice cream!

3

The Lost Silver Spike

Beany had never yet got used to the fact that her father, Martie Malone, always met discouragement and disappointment smilingly, almost jovially. And that victory always sobered him. As though the fighter in him was so braced for losing that he found triumph unsettling.

It was dusk when the telephone call Martie Malone had been waiting for the whole afternoon came through.

Mary Fred had waited in vain for a call from old Baggy. And so Mary Fred still had one foot in heaven and one mired in Harkness' chem lab.

Martie Malone took his telephone call with one foot on the three-cornered telephone chair, with Red watching his face for assurance. He made enigmatic answers, "They did, huh? . . . Hm'mm. . . . Yes, I know. . . . Well, thanks."

It was dusk when Elizabeth rocked little Martie in his washed-out pink sleepers. Even downstairs Beany could

26

sense the rhythmic creak of her rocker and the sing-song cadence of her voice. Little Martie's favorite song was "Red Wing," provided Elizabeth did a little revising—"The breeze is sighing. . . ." But if she ever absently added, "The nightbirds crying," he would jerk upright to correct vehemently, "No—they are *not*—"

"That's right, I forgot," Elizabeth would retract hastily, and sing it, "The nightbirds are *not* crying." It was quite all right for Red Wing to be "weeping her heart away" in the last line because the little boy's vocabulary, to date, did not include "weeping."

It was dusk, and from the boulevard a half-block away came the rushing swish of after-the-game traffic, the hoarse yells of victory from cars decked with waving purple and white streamers. Harkness High had won its second football game. Beany tried not to think, If I'd gone with Norbett I'd be in his red car yelling, "You're low—we're high! Harkness High!" Instead she was clearing the table of its sickening clutter so that they could have dinner. Once her foot struck the ocarina that Jock had dropped in excited indifference.

Her father came out into the kitchen. "Beany," he said gravely, "I've won. The city council passed the law I've been battling for. From now on anyone caught breaking traffic laws will have his car impounded. From now on anyone without an up-to-date brake and light sticker on his car will have it impounded. That ought to cut down accidents. Whew!" he added with a tired heave. "It's been a long, hard battle."

She said "Congratulations," but she was thinking of Norbett saying, "All the young people call him Killjoy Malone." She went on, pulling the half-guttered and limp candles out of the cake, prying the melted, now solidified, globules of pink wax out of the icing.

Her father mused, "I can't get over what a well-rounded cake you made out of Johnny's lopsided job. Your hands are capable, Beany. How old are you now?"

"Sixteen," she reminded him.

His smile was just an older, tireder edition of Johnny's appealing one. He came over and put his arm around Beany's seersucker shoulders. "Beany, I'm about to dump something else into your capable hands. If you say the word. Doc Hunter has been hounding me to get to Arizona before cold weather hits. Says the pneumonia left me too bedraggled to stand a winter here. But I couldn't pull out right in the middle of my fight—"

He saw the startled, stricken look that lifted the freckles across her nose into bold relief. "Just for a few months, child. Just for a build-up. Just if you think you can manage."

"What—what do the others say?"

"I'm telling you first, Beany. Because all the time I've been thinking it over, I could see the biggest load falling on you. Elizabeth has her heart and hands full. Either waiting and worrying about Don, or building a life with him when he comes back. Mary Fred got thrown out of her stride last spring when I was sick. I want her to catch up on her senior credits so she can have a real fling at college and all college means. And then Johnny—"

"Johnny's got Emerson Worth's book on his hands—"

"—and Emerson Worth," he added. "And time that's running short. . . . What do you say, Beany? Could you go on, filling in the Malones' mistakes, just as you did with Johnny's lopsided cake?"

Beany couldn't answer for the sudden choked feeling.

As though her father had said, "Into thy hands, Beany,
I leave the happiness of the Malones." . . . Oh yes, she
thought, oh yes! I'll keep them all from making mistakes.
(If I'd put a little more flour in Johnny's cake it wouldn't
have fallen.) I'll keep all the Malones from sticking their
necks out. We Malones need to lock hearts and doors. We're
unfair to ourselves. Beany saw herself, like a picket guard-
ing the portals of the Malone home, bearing the placard,
"The Malones are unfair to themselves."

She finally managed to say, "Yes, I'll look after them."
But she had a feeling that she had made a sacred, yet grim
vow, "I do solemnly promise to protect the Malones."

Her father pulled her to him by one of her braids,
"Beany, our ballast," he said fondly.

But alas for Beany's vow, born out of her own hurt
desolation, her protective loyalty for the family. Alas for
her thinking it would be easy to lock Malone hearts or
doors.

They sat down to the dinner Mrs. No-complaint Adams
had left in a slow oven for them. Johnny said, "There's all
that ice cream from the party for dessert," and Beany
answered heavily, "I don't want any." I don't ever want
to see pink ice cream again, she thought with revulsion that
was close to nausea.

Beany was bringing in the teapot when she almost
collided with an old man who had come wandering in the
front door and on through the house.

Old Emerson Worth stood in the dining-room door,
chilled and faltering. One of his shaky hands held his
black hat, which had aged to a limp, greenish black. His
white hair was soft as silk floss and, like Johnny's, needed

a barber's shears. His other hand gripped his gold-headed malacca cane.

That cane and his white silk muffler were Emerson's buoys against life's defeat—the drab, dark disorder of his room in a cheap rooming house, his worn-through shoes, his gaunt emptiness and shakiness. Again and again the Malones had tried to "do for him" by pulling him under their own wide roof, but Emerson's pride was bitter and touchy.

He stood there, like a wind-battered and bewildered old rooster. Even his gray, out-jutting eyebrows had a worried fierceness. "It's lost—the silver spike is lost," he appealed to them. "The governor is going to pound it in at the train celebration. He's waiting to have it handed to him—" He was frantically pawing through the odds and ends out of his pockets—a penknife with a cracked pearl handle, short copy pencils, a length of worn shoelace—

"Beany," Johnny said in a sibilant whisper. "Make some coffee strong enough to float the lost railroad spike."

Someone got the old man to the table, set a dish of split-pea soup, seasoned with chunky sausages, before him. While Beany made the coffee, Johnny was saying, "Poor old Emerson, and the lost silver spike. It really *was* missing. Emerson was a boy of eight and he came down from Georgetown for the celebration of the first train into Denver. The miners of Georgetown were to present the silver spike to the governor to pound in, when they laid the last rail, but it seems— Beany, I'd put in more coffee."

"I know *you* would," she said undisturbed, as she turned the flame high under the percolator. "It seems the miners what?"

"—it seems these fellows did a little too much celebrating

and, at the ceremony, there was a wild confusion to find either the spike or the fellow that had it—"

"What did happen to the silver spike?" Beany asked.

"I don't know," Johnny said. "That's one of the things I've got to get out of Emerson when his mind is clear."

Beany walked in with the coffee just in time to hear her father saying, "Emerson, I'm glad you showed up. I want to ask a favor of you. I have to leave for Arizona to soak up some sun. And I wondered if I could get you to stay here with the children while I'm gone. We'll have that extra room and bed going begging. I'd go with a clearer conscience if you were here."

Oh no; Beany wanted to cry out. No—that's just what we mustn't do. You're not fooling me or any of us—except poor old Emerson Worth. You're just finding a way to save his pride and still get him out of that pitiful little old cold room of his, with the books spilling out of packing cases, and the lumpy bed. With him here Johnny won't think of anything but *Our City Has Deep Roots*. But they aren't Johnny's roots.

She looked hopefully at the old man. Surely he would see through Martie Malone's tactful ruse. But Emerson Worth's lofty smile was that of one conferring a favor even though it means a great sacrifice. It was the smile Emerson Worth, great newspaperman, would bestow upon Martie Malone, a struggling reporter. He had quite forgotten these last years when Martie had to use his whole weight to keep him at a desk in the most obscure corner in the *Call's* editorial room.

"Well now, Martie," the old man said, "I guess I can help you out. I can arrange my affairs so that I can stay here and look after the children."

Beany's soul groaned.

That same evening after the dishes were done, she went up to Johnny's cluttered room.

Johnny sat in the swivel chair in front of his desk. The swivel chair was the kind that tipped scaringly far back if you relaxed in it; Johnny, alone, knew just how far back to lean in it without tempting providence. Johnny's desk had once been a blackish mission table. He had given it a coat of blue paint, but now it was nicked and chipped with hard use until the dark coat showed beneath. And Johnny's typewriter had a rakish way of jumping an extra space or two—"Like a trotting horse breaking into a singlefoot," Johnny excused it.

"Johnny," Beany began earnestly, "I don't mind having Emerson here and feeding him up good—"

"Lordy, did you see the poor old coot put away three plates of soup tonight?" Johnny said with a fond smile. "He's never so wandery when his stomach is full."

"—but look, Johnny, why don't you just forget Emerson's book? You're a senior now and all the school is looking to you to—to be outstanding. Miss Hewlitt asked me the other day if you had any ideas for the mid-year play. Because—well, you said yourself that fate didn't grind any slower than publishers. Even if a publisher took Emerson's book, it'd be a long time before it was published. And you know Dr. Hunter said his heart was like a leaky bicycle pump."

"I know," Johnny sighed; he leaned back, managed to catch himself in time. "I know," he repeated unhappily, hooking his long legs under the table by way of anchor. "And that's what's haunting me. But I'd like to see Emerson have his final blaze of glory. And he's got a message for all the folks who never gave a thought to how the city was born—you know, like that Miss what's-her-name starting the first school—"

"Indiana Sopris," Beany prompted. "And she rounded up the kids and started a school in a blacksmith shop. But what I'm saying—"

"—and the train's coming," Johnny pursued, "and how they had to fight and shove the roadbed over every foot of buffalo wallows and sandcreeks—"

"Never mind the buffalo wallows," Beany insisted. "What I'm saying is that I'm afraid it will be too late."

"Emerson and his lost silver spike," Johnny mused. "It isn't the silver spike he's looking for. It's the dream he has lost; the dream he's had of telling people about those early days."

"But an old man in his eighties," Beany went on inexorably, "doesn't have many years ahead—or even one, sometimes. And this is your senior year—and there's the school play and everyone expects you to bob up with some swell idea."

Johnny's feet came down with a thump. His eyes took on a far-away raptness. "By golly, Beany, I'd forgot about that mid-year play. I just thought of something. Gee, thanks. I'm going to talk to Miss Hewlitt—I believe I'll telephone her right now. Gangway, chit."

Beany gladly gave him gangway and went to her own room.

Beany's room was the smallest one of the five upstairs bedrooms. It had been intended as merely the nursery adjunct of the two-room suite which had been Mother's and Father's while their mother lived. But after her death Martie Malone had turned the two connecting rooms over to the two older girls and had moved his black leather chair and his desk-bookcase into the north bedroom.

Beany, the youngest and last occupant of the small nursery room, had clung to it, even though Mary Fred called it a stuffy little stall, and she and Elizabeth constantly urged Beany to share with them the big room with the corner fireplace, and the adjoining room, which they always called "the porch" because of its three walls of windows. From the porch a Dutch door opened onto a balcony where Johnny in winter used to make snowballs and pelt them at Beany in the yard, where Elizabeth in summer used to give the baby Martie sunbaths. (But now the door had to be kept locked against the little fellow's getting out and climbing the railing.) Mary Fred, the fresh-air addict, slept on "the porch." Elizabeth and little Martie occupied the warmer room.

Beany loved her little stall. She had redone it herself, following directions in a decorating magazine for just such a one-windowed small room. She had saved and bought all those yards of yellow plaid gingham and made the ruffled window curtains and the skirt for the dressing table. The little drawer under the skirt always stuck, but Beany didn't mind that. "Lift the sun out of the sky and bring it into your room," the decorating article had blithely promised. Beany's pale blue ceiling, the smiling curtains, the white oval rug by her bed, did bring the sun into Beany's room—and into her heart.

Tonight she stood in front of the mirror, bordered by snapshots, and took out the one of Jock and Lorna. That blur of white was her big rabbit, Frank, which Lorna held and which had squirmed as the camera clicked. Beany dropped the picture into the wastebasket. Again the broken edges of hurt rubbed together. . . . It wouldn't happen again. She'd see to that. And she'd see that the other Malones didn't lay themselves open to disappointment and hurt.

She heard Johnny's buoyant feet leap up the stairs after his telephone conversation with Miss Hewlitt. She heard his enthusiastic attack on his typewriter. That was another reason she loved her room. It was at the head of the stairs so that every footstep had to pass her door. It was like a finger on the pulse of the Malone home.

She reached for her Latin book and Monday's assignment. Beany, the protector of the Malones, had veered Johnny away from thinking about bringing a blaze of glory to Emerson Worth. She had started Johnny thinking about bringing a blaze of glory to Johnny Malone, senior at Harkness.

So Beany thought.

4

Revenge Is Sweet!

Mrs. No-complaint Adams worked the first half of the day for the Judge Buell family of three—the judge, his wife, and their son, Carlton. She came to the Malone home at twelve-thirty and worked until four-thirty. Mrs. Adams never lost a chance to impress upon the Malones how grateful they should be that she gave them a half-day when so many others were clamoring for her incomparable services.

Mrs. No-complaint had many complaints on her side. Her latest and, to date, strongest was the coming of Emerson Worth. Like Beany, Mrs. Adams wasn't happy over his occupying Martie Malone's bedroom (even though he slept in the guest room until Martie Malone should leave on Tuesday).

The Malones got breakfast themselves. Beany, the squeezer of oranges. Johnny, the custodian of the toaster. "First you burn it, then you scrape it," was Johnny's recipe. The first one to reach the kitchen put on the coffee percolator. Elizabeth, busy with dressing the small Martie during breakfast-getting, washed the breakfast dishes. "I tremble for us if we ever left the oatmeal kettle for Mrs. No-complaint," Elizabeth always said.

On the morning of the Tuesday that followed Beany's sad and disillusioning Saturday, Beany came into the kitchen to find Mary Fred already there, studying chemistry. That, alone, emphasized the dire urgency of Mary Fred's chem.

For Mary Fred was the sleepy-head of the Malones. She was always saying, "Now I'll get up early and do—" and then barely scramble down in time to bolt her breakfast and be off. "The Nitrogen Family and I are gathered together," she imparted this morning.

There was always a scurry among the young Malones to be the first to get the *Morning Call,* though, of course, the minute Martie Malone came on the scene, he was given priority. Sometimes the paper was thumped nicely against their front door. Sometimes—especially on rainy or snowy mornings—it had to be hunted for and extracted from the bridal-wreath bushes which bordered the porch.

On this Tuesday morning Johnny came into the kitchen with the paper while Beany whacked oranges in half and thought, I wonder if Norbett will be in typing class today. He wasn't there yesterday. Beany never knew just which mood Norbett might be in. Some days he sat aloof, scowling at his copy with no notice of anyone—not even the very good speller sitting next to him who hoped she would be interrupted. Some days he would be jocular, swaggering, full of bright wisecracks. That was the show-off Norbett, man-about-town Norbett. Then there were days when he seemed to reach out of a lonely, unhappy inadequacy— "Is there a plural to *strata?*" he would ask Beany.

"*Strata is* plural," she would answer happily. "The singular is *stratum.*"

"Johnny, the toast!" Beany yelled, as a wisp of odorous smoke ascended to the ceiling. Johnny grabbed for it absently, his eyes still on the morning paper, without even hearing Mary Fred's, "I should be studying the Carbon Family." Even as he flipped the blackened slice out of the toaster, he was saying, "Oh my bent crutch, Beany—look at this, will you?"

On the front page of the *Morning Call* was the picture of a thin-featured boy with dark, challenging eyes. It was the picture Norbett Rhodes had had taken for graduation when he had no doubts of being graduated. And under the picture heavy print read, "Nephew of our traffic manager, N. J. Rhodes, is first to be penalized by new traffic law. Story on page five."

With a half of an orange in her hand, Beany's shoulders brushed Johnny's as they read the details on page five. Mary Fred stopped her scribbling of formulas to read it. Norbett Rhodes had been arrested for going forty-five on a thirty-mile-limit boulevard. His car did not have a brake and light sticker. Judge Buell had reprimanded him, fined him, and impounded his car for ninety days. Norbett Rhodes held the dubious distinction of being the first to feel the teeth of the new law Martie Malone had fought to have passed.

Johnny said generously, "Gosh, that's tough!"

Beany murmured, "He just had it painted—he had it painted red." She thought, oh, now he'll hate us Malones more than ever . . . But I don't care. I decided last Saturday I didn't care about Norbett hating the Malones . . .

Mary Fred said, "I hope he won't be in chem when I'm there doing make-up today. He'll be in a sourer mood than usual. And he always comes in a very clabbered state. He has the work table next to mine. He gets old Baggy so edgy, making his sneering remarks about the uselessness of chem. That Norbett and his grudges! He keeps himself thin, carrying them around."

The telephone was ringing. Beany answered it. Now that Emerson Worth was under their own green-shingled roof, Johnny didn't make such flying dashes for the black instrument.

It was the owner-manager of the *Call* asking for Martie Malone. "If he isn't down yet," the voice said, "take a message for him. Let's see—he's leaving town tonight?"

"Yes, he plans to leave this evening on the plane."

"That's what I thought. Well, tell him we'd like him to whip out an editorial on this Rhodes' nephew affair before he leaves. It's right up his alley." The manager of the *Call* chuckled, "I don't imagine N. J. Rhodes is enjoying his breakfast this morning. Just tell Martie, if he can find time, we'd like a sizzler on it before he leaves."

"I'll tell him," Beany said. Red was waiting at the telephone as usual, waiting to know if he should wag his tail or keep it at half-mast. Something in Beany's voice decided him on the latter. Beany's hand dropped onto his head. Funny, she thought, Norbett's hair is that same chestnut brown. . . .

She started up the stairs toward the sound of an electric razor and her father's singing of "Kathleen Mavourneen—the gray dawn is breaking—" The fragrance of percolating coffee seeped through the house. But to Beany, going up the stairs, it was just a brown, unappetizing smell.

N. J. Rhodes wasn't the only one who wouldn't enjoy his breakfast this morning.

In the excitement of the morning Beany forgot her school locker key.

The sophomore lockers, even as the junior and senior, were assigned alphabetically. The girl who had the locker next to Beany Malone's was Kay Maffley. Beany hadn't, as yet, a chum at Harkness High. The girl she had walked to and from junior high and eaten lunches with had moved away. Beany knew most of her classmates, having gone through grammar school and junior high with many of them, but she felt the need of a *best* friend to share her candy bars, confidences, art pencils, woes, and gym shoes with.

Maybe it would be Kay Maffley. Kay Maffley was a new girl at Harkness. Kay, like Beany's sister, Elizabeth, had a magazine-cover loveliness. Her soft cascade of hair hung longer than shoulder length; it was the color of well-pulled taffy and had the same sheen. Her face never had more than a gentle flush, her lips never more than a half-smile—a studied, fixed half-smile.

The very fact that Kay Maffley walked alone through the teeming halls and ate alone in the bedlam that was the lunchroom made Beany long to take her under her sturdy wing. But did Kay want a sturdy and friendly wing?

The first week of school Beany, swinging her sack of lunch, caught up with Kay on the stairs. "How about eating lunch with me, Kay? I eat with four or five others, but I thought maybe we two—"

Beany was so sure Kay was going to say, "Oh, I'd love to," for her smile quivered with eagerness. She even started,

"Oh, Beany—" and then she said remotely, "Well, thanks, Beany, but I don't bring my lunch. I buy it."

Beany was rebuffed and puzzled.

The girl students at Harkness fell into three groups— the studes, the queens, and the mop-squeezers. The studes, of course, were the grinds, usually spectacled, usually serious, who carried weighty stacks of books from one classroom to another. They always had their notebooks in on the date specified. Before a math test a stude never had to ask someone frantically, "What is it about the minus sign in a parenthesis? Don't you change it to a plus or something?"

The queens—sometimes called wrens or eye-happys— were the girls who had dates galore. They lolled about the halls and on the steps, talking to football fellows or other big shots. They were the envied. It wasn't that their clothes were different, because sweaters of rainbow hue with plaid or plain skirts were almost uniform. Perhaps the queens wore them with that extra and indefinable dash. Perhaps it was the extra cockiness of their own lure.

And the mop-squeezers were the doers. They scurried about on committees to get competitive prices on ices and orchestras for the proms, where the queens danced every dance, with never a thought about such mundane details. The mop-squeezers frilled the edges of miles of crepe paper for school parties in the gym. They got down sherbet cups from Homemaking, and hunted them up for returning, often finding them left carelessly by the queens on windowsills or stairs.

Not that all mop-squeezers didn't have fun and dates. But the queens were school royalty, picking and choosing.

Beany was a mop-squeezer, just as Mary Fred had been

before her. Beany had no illusions about herself. She liked making cookies in Homemaking for a Mothers' Day Tea and talking over programs for Miss Hewlitt's Literary Society. . . . Of course there was that dream of hers of dancing so many dances with Norbett Rhodes at the Friday Social Hours that everyone would say, "H'mm, look what goes with Norbett and Beany! Norbett isn't eating his heart out for Mary Fred any more." . . . There *had* been that dream, Beany kept reminding herself. But now—now she wasn't sticking her neck out for trouble.

Kay Maffley, at first glance—with the loveliness of her taffy-colored hair and the just-rightness of her clothes— would seem to be a queen. But queens had a preening awareness of the other sex. And Kay hadn't.

Unable to classify her, the school labeled her Frozen-face. At school's end they muttered to each other, "The ice-cream wagon awaits Frozen-face." For every day at the foot of the school's thirty-two steps a car, the color of vanilla ice cream, its chromium glinting in the fall sun, waited with a woman at the wheel who looked like a slightly older sister of Kay's. Taffy-colored hair, turquoise sweater on the days Kay wore a turquoise sweater. Red, sheep-lined coat on the days Kay wore her red, sheep-lined coat.

So on this Tuesday morning, when Norbett Rhodes' picture was splashed over the first page of the *Call* and Beany forgot her locker key, she appealed to Kay, her locker neighbor. "Could I put my coat in your locker?"

Again the immobility of Kay's face broke and warmed. "Sure, Beany—why, sure—" as though she were hungry for a girl asking, "Kay, can I share—?" But then she added stiffly, "Only I have to leave right after sixth hour. I mean I can't wait around for you to get it."

Later that afternoon Carlton Buell fell into step beside Beany as they traversed the hallway that led to typing and to Shop. Beany mused, "I wonder if Norbett Rhodes will be in typing today. He wasn't there yesterday."

"Yesterday," Carlton said, "was his busy day. Police officers, traffic court, and facing my father, Judge Buell." Carlton added with a rueful chuckle, "You'd better *hope* he isn't there. I saw him this morning, and when I started to say, 'Hi Rhodes,' he gave me a look that would wither a fall aster. The sentences of the father are visited on the children, I take it."

"And the crusades of the father are visited on the children," Beany said, even more ruefully.

Carlton Buell, with his stubby blond hair, his shy, unassuming grin, was a comfortable person. "Don't tell any of the teachers my father is a judge," he used to warn Johnny, "or they'll expect me to be smarter than I am." To Beany, he was just Johnny's shadow. As Lila Sears was Mary Fred's shadow. She would never think of using freckle cream because she sat next to Carlton Buell in class.

She wasn't sure whether she was relieved or disappointed to find Norbett's typewriter shrouded and the chair tilted forward on the desk. But Norbett had *been* there. As Beany pulled off her typewriter cover, she found a note on its roll in Norbett's uneven typing. ("You should learn rhythm in your touch, Norbett," the teacher was always reminding him.)

Beany read the note through twice:

So there is much rejoicing in the Malone camp over catching N. J. Rhodes' nephew in the trap. Okay, crow your fill over it. Just as Killjoy Malone warned all the kids in advance that he was out to get them, so I'm warning you. I won't rest till I can rub any or all the Malone nose's in the dust. Revenge is sweet!

Shakily Beany inserted the paper in her typewriter and added a short paragraph to it. "The plural of nose is noses—no apostrophe." Almost without mental volition her fingers typed on, "I'm sorry about your red car."

But that wouldn't do. Not for Beany who was keeping her heart under lock and key. She shifted to a capital X and X'd it out heavily, leaving only the part about the plural of nose.

She slid it under the black cover of Norbett's machine.

5

Those Who Carry the Banner

Kay was waiting with fidgety impatience to give Beany her reversible at the end of sixth hour. Then Kay banged shut her locker and hurried off alone.

When other students were called for, they usually loaded up the car with friends and dropped them off. Beany would have been thankful for a lift this afternoon. Father was leaving on a plane this evening. Kay Maffley lived at the Park Gate Apartment Hotel which faced the park; that was where Norbett Rhodes lived with his aunt and uncle. It would have been only a swing across the park and a few added blocks to the Malone home. But Kay walked out of the big doors just ahead of Beany and down the steps without ever a "Come on, Beany, we'll drop you off."

Father's bags were only partially packed. Mrs. No-complaint's iron was hurrying over the last of his shirts. Johnny had gone from school to Emerson Worth's rooming house and brought out Emerson's few belongings. It was hard for

Beany not to feel a residue of resentment to see Emerson Worth taking over Father's room. It was so entirely Father's—from the ever-present pipe smell and the litter of short copy sheets to the winged black leather chair, its cushions hollowed out from his weight, the arms scuffed and scabby from his restless thrumming fingers.

Elizabeth sat on the window seat, mending the torn pocket on Father's sweater. Father's breast pockets, as well as Johnny's, were always a little the worse for Red's exuberant greetings. Red acted with gentlemanly decorum with the feminine sex, but he always leaped up, in paws-on-their-chest ecstasy, when Father or Johnny returned.

While Father waited for Mary Fred to return from the cleaner's with his topcoat, he distributed a thick pack of penny postals. "A penny for your thoughts," he said; each of the four children was to send him one every week to keep him in touch with all that happened on Barberry Street.

Mrs. Adams brought up his folded shirts and Father stood holding them, looking helplessly at his full suitcase. "Beany," he appealed, "just how can we get my bedroom slippers and these in? As much as I've traveled, I've never learned to pack."

"Let me try," she said.

She was repacking the suitcase and Johnny was cramming the razor and shaving cream into a slipper, when Father said, "Johnny, I've been putting off a bit of before-I-go preaching. Not too long a sermon. You could say it in one sentence—no, two. One, those who carry the banner must walk carefully. Two, and the family of anyone who carries the banner should watch their step."

Johnny's grin was understanding, reassuring. "Meaning

that Johnny Malone better watch the speed limits when he drives his jalopy by name of Insomnia. And get a brake and light sticker before driving same. I thought of that when I saw Norbett's picture this morning. Gosh, the *Tribune* would run an extra edition if they ever got anything on us Malones. Don't worry, pop. That's why I'm not driving Insomnia. Got to have some work done on the brakes. But I'll edge it up to Mac's garage on the boulevard and have him check it over and give me my sticker. Insomnia will sit and sulk in our garage until then."

"Fine, son."

Beany looked around the room. "And your portable, Father. Is it ready?"

"Pull the copy out, Beany. That's the editorial. The *Call* is sending a special messenger out for it."

Beany pulled the typed pages out. A sentence or two leaped out at her. "—not only charity should begin at home, but a respect for traffic laws should begin in the home of our traffic manager. . . such young drivers a menace to our families . . ."

She stood, holding it, her unhappy eyes skimming over it.

Martie Malone asked, "What's the matter, Beany? Doesn't it sound all right?"

"But you've—you've already said so much about young people and their driving. They call you Killjoy Malone— they think you've got it in for them."

He stared at her thoughtfully for a long minute. Slowly he reached out and took the sheets from her hand. "Beany, I'm glad you told me that." Thoughtfully he crumpled the copy sheets of tomorrow's editorial and threw them toward the full wastebasket. "Thanks, honey. That one did sort of

rub salt on the sore. I know the editorial I want to write."
He looked at his wrist watch. "If someone will bring me a
tray with a bite to eat on it, I'll pound out a new one. Scram,
kids, while I get busy."

The cab from the airfield came sooner than they thought.
There was the scurry of good-by, with all the laughing,
choked nothings people say when their hearts are full.
Father's special smile, his special hug and thump on the
back for each one—except Johnny, who got a squeezed
handclasp that was really a caress and a blessing.

Father said to Beany as he squirmed into his topcoat
and patted the pockets to be reassured that his can of tobacco and pipe were going with him, "Beany, I wrote my
editorial, but it needs cleaning up and retyping. I believe
you can do it, and have it ready when the *Call* sends for it."

How empty the house seemed as the yellow cab whirred
off!

While Emerson Worth dozed mutteringly in Martie
Malone's leather chair, Beany retyped Martie Malone's
editorial for Wednesday's *Morning Call*—that editorial
which was to be reprinted in newspapers all over the country, even published in Digest magazines. Safety councils
in other cities were to give out copies of it. Schools were
to make it compulsory reading for students in Citizenship.

It was called an "Open Letter to Young People and Returned G.I.'s." A talky, friendly, even tender letter, which
started,

I am sorry you young people think of me as Killjoy
Malone. Perhaps it will take a longer view before you
can think of me as Killgrief Malone. Do you think that
having your car impounded is the worst thing that

could happen to you? Then follow up with me the tragic aftermath of just one month of traffic accidents in our city. Multiply it by twelve; multiply it by all the other cities.

He told of a young man who had hit and killed a little girl—a young man who would never be young again. Not a night had he been able to drop off to sleep without feeling that same bump of a child's body jolting his car. In his waking hours, in his sleeping hours, he was to hear always the screams of the child's mother. It was the albatross he would carry through life.

Martie Malone listed them in his "Open Letter." The pitiful, heart-twisting, body-wrecking, life-wrecking statistics. It ended,

I worked for the passing of this law because I thought of it not as a net to catch reckless drivers, but as a friendly, restraining hand that would warn, "Slow down, young drivers, careless drivers. Lives are precious—yours, and the other fellow's."

Beany folded it slowly and put it into the *Morning Call* envelope. Some of its amiable wisdom, its lack of pettiness, had soaked into her. And suddenly she longed for Norbett to have the sting taken out of his rancor.

She suddenly longed to say to him, "Norbett, read Father's editorial in tomorrow's paper." And, on that sudden, warm impulse, she went to the telephone and dialed the Park Gate Apartment Hotel and asked for the Rhodes apartment.

The hotel switchboard operator demanded with crisp wariness, "Who is calling, please?"

Beany said awkwardly, "Why, I—I just wanted to talk—to Norbett—"

The operator said, "I'm sorry, but I have orders not to ring the Rhodes apartment." Beany only said, "Oh!" Perhaps the operator sensed her deflation and confusion, for she added confidentially, "They're pretty furious over all the publicity in the paper. But if you want to leave your name—"

Beany even started to say, "It's Beany Ma—" But suddenly she broke off. She had bumped into the rough wall of the enemy camp. She didn't dare scale the wall and meet their contempt and fury. She hadn't realized that in calling Norbett Rhodes she would be entering the Rhodes camp, waving a white flag.

All her warming eagerness seeped away. "Well—thanks—I—well, never mind."

She replaced the telephone receiver.

6

Last Stand of the Buffalo

On a drizzly Tuesday, a week from the Tuesday when Norbett Rhodes' picture had been front-paged in the *Call*, Beany pushed through the crowd that rimmed the school bulletin board at Harkness High.

The notice that caused the ripple of excitement had been put up by the drama teacher.

ALL STUDENTS PLEASE MEET SIXTH HOUR IN THE AUDITO-
RIUM TO DISCUSS OUR MID-YEAR PLAY. THE SCHOOL WILL
DECIDE BY VOTE ON THE PREFERRED PLAY.

Beany read the notice with mixed emotions. Here was Johnny's chance to shine as a gifted senior. Johnny had some play idea up his sleeve. The night following Emerson Worth's arrival, when she had mentioned the mid-year play, Johnny's dark eyes had taken on a creative gleam. And sure enough, Beany had seen him in engrossed conference with Miss Hewlitt, English Lit teacher and Johnny's backer—his spurrer-on.

But so had Norbett Rhodes something up his sleeve for
the big mid-year show. Beany knew, because just yesterday,
when the typing teacher had reminded him that he hadn't
as yet turned in his Control Drill exercise, he had answered
loftily that he was typing out some ideas for a school opera.

Beany had been typing her Control Drill paragraph.
Every fifth-hour typing since Martie Malone's "Open
Letter" had appeared in the *Call*, she had hoped for an
opportunity to ask Norbett if he had seen it. But Norbett
had given her none. Even yesterday she had hoped for
an opening all the time her fingers typed, "A salesman's
cause is lost as soon as he starts to use sarcasm. His samples
may satisfy, . . ."

She made a mistake on the *y*. Maybe she could ask to
borrow Norbett's eraser. But that was when Miss Meigs
spoke to him about his Control Drill and he answered that
he was typing ideas for an opera. He attacked the keys,
pounding with such pent-up fury and vigor that the teacher
reminded him, "Rhythm, Norbett, rhythm. Don't fight
your typewriter or it'll fight back." . . . Rhythm, Norbett, rhythm, Beany thought. If you wouldn't fight the
world so, it wouldn't fight back. . . .

Coming out of the lunchroom that next day, Tuesday,
when all the school was talkily excited about the choosing
of the play, Beany saw Johnny over in the senior division.
Her sisterly soul groaned. If only she had *made* Johnny get
his long shock of hair cut. He'd get up in front of the whole
school, looking like a Russian refugee. And he *would* be
wearing that sport shirt with one breast pocket partially
ripped off by Red's exuberant greetings.

Beany tried to get within hailing distance of him after

fourth-hour class, but Johnny was lost swiftly in the noisy tide of passing classes.

Kay Maffley was at her open locker when Beany delved into hers to get out her typing book. Kay's back was to Beany while Kay pounded a powder puff over her face. Beany asked, "Kay, you take Glee Club next hour, don't you?"

"Yes."

"You know my brother Johnny, don't you?"

"Yes, I know him. I sit next to him."

Kay kept her back to Beany, but Beany enjoined anxiously, "Well look, Kay, will you tell him something? Tell him to wear his leather jacket when he gets up in aud—and to button it so that mucky-looking sport shirt doesn't show. Red—he's our dog—always runs to meet him and jumps on him and that's what tore his pocket. My goodness, you can all but see Red's pawmarks on Johnny's front."

"Okay, I'll tell him. What kind of a dog—is Red?"

Her voice had such a wan thinness that Beany moved closer. Kay's back was still to her but she could see Kay's face in the small mirror fitted inside the locker door. Kay's reflected blue eyes had a tell-tale pink murkiness. Beany said in alarm, "Kay, you're crying! What's the matter?"

Kay half turned. A tremor of sobs—like a shiver—passed through her, crimped her tight lips. And before she could uncrimp them the warning bell clanged about them. The very demanding "Hurry" of the warning bell. Each one had to go running—Kay to Glee Club, Beany to typing.

Excitement made the full auditorium like a humming teakettle.

The drama teacher had to wait a full minute for the

rustling whispers to subside. Beany could sense the two pulls—Johnny Malone; Norbett Rhodes.

The drama teacher's name was Melinda Page. She was a young, alert, tweed-suited person with a swinging stride and a voice deep and beautifully modulated. The school in fond admiration and no disrespect called her by her first name, Melinda.

Even though Melinda's opening speech was the usual one about Harkness High's reputation for putting on unusual entertainment, the audience clapped lustily as vent for their fidgety impatience. Two seniors, Melinda explained, had ideas to lay before them and it would be up to the student body to make their choice.

Norbett Rhodes stood up. (Norbett's hair, the same shade as an Irish setter's, had recently felt a barber's shears, Beany noted.) Norbett occupied a unique position at Harkness. He was their man-about-town. As school reporter for the city paper, *The Tribune*, he called other reporters, who were just names to the rest of the school, by their first names. After his singing the lead in last year's opera, he had been asked to sing some of the songs over a local radio station.

The sympathy of the school was with him because of Professor Bagley's unwavering grimness in keeping him from graduation last year. Other students, in quaking fear of old Baggy, reveled vicariously in Norbett's feud with him. Even the fact that Norbett had been caught driving forty-five on a thirty-mile boulevard, with the penalty of an impounded car, added to his luster with the students—though not with the faculty. Decidedly not with the faculty!

Beany, sitting in the second row of the sophomore section, could see Norbett's nervous hands shaking as he shuffled the notes made on the Woodstock typewriter next to hers. A rush of sympathy filled her. Norbett laid the notes on the piano and thrust his hands into his pockets with a sure-of-himself swagger.

Norbett told them that the time was right for a jolly, big-cast opera. Look at the success of *Oklahoma!* and *Carmen Jones—*

The girl next to Beany nudged her with a low giggle. "Could be Norbett wants to strut his stuff in his scarlet-lined cape."

Norbett went on. Why not take a leaf from *Carmen Jones* and modernize a sure-fire opera? *Romeo and Juliet* would be a corker. They could get some swell gag lines out of all that family-feud business.

Oh gosh, Beany thought! Oh gosh, dynamite! So that's what Norbett had up his sleeve! The Capulets and the Montagues. The Malones and the Rhodeses. Oh, couldn't he get some swell gag lines out of it! This would be a wonderful way for him to rub Malone noses (not nose's) in the dirt.

She looked fearfully about. Didn't all those packed, excited students see the irony of it? But no, evidently not. The school saw only a farced-up, jazzed-up comedy with Shakespeare's flowery and stilted phrasing made ludicrous. Beany was thankful for that; thankful that no one knew what went on under her coral-pink sweater when Norbett asked her help in spelling.

Norbett went on. They could use a big cast by having a ball scene. "Of course we'd modernize it," he said vaguely. "The fighting wouldn't be with swords."

Norbett sat down amid tumultuous applause.

And then Johnny Malone took the platform.

Beany squirmed with longing to say, "Johnny, push the hair out of your eyes." And what had happened to the message she had sent him, via Kay? For he wore no leather jacket to hide his flapping pocket and the area smudged by Red's fond paws.

Johnny hadn't any notes. He had only his nice, generous, slightly apologetic grin which pulled them all into warm cahoots with him. That, and his own earnestness. "I've got a different idea—and if you like it, swell. This is it. I guess most of you know about this old fellow, Emerson Worth, who has a dream of giving you the story of this town getting born. I've been helping him on his manuscript for years. We call it *Our City Has Deep Roots.*"

In his eagerness Johnny walked out to the edge of the stage. "And then my sister, Beany—I mean Catherine—" with a flash of smile that said, "Excuse me, teachers,"— "pointed out to me the other evening that time was running out—and pretty fast on the old man. So I figured he could realize his dream if we could put the material on the stage. Maybe it would take too long to get in book form, but this way—"

But Johnny, Beany wanted to cry out, I was just trying to wean you away from the lost railroad spike, and Cherry Creek floods, and last stands of the buffalo. I didn't mean for it to backfire on me like this. I wanted you to be Johnny Malone, outstanding senior in your own right—not Johnny Malone crusading for Emerson Worth's dream of a lifetime.

"—not anything in the orthodox three-act play style," Johnny was saying. "But something like *The Eve of St. Mark*—or *The Glass Menagerie*—or *Our Town.* We'd have a narrator who carries it along. 'The place is here,' he'd say. 'The time is memory.' We'd run the scenes off swiftly—like flashbacks on a screen—"

Beany saw Miss Hewlitt sitting anxiously upright, her lips twitching in her weathered face, like a mother whose precious child is speaking a piece. Beany saw Melinda's face tilted, her eyes half-closed, as though her dramatic eyes were projecting Johnny's thoughts on a stage, testing them. What was it Norbett had said that Saturday (it seemed so long ago) when she had almost gone to the football game with him? "Johnny will get up with some half-baked idea and have them all eating out of his hand."

"Old Emerson Worth," Johnny was skimming along, "came out here when he was three in a covered wagon and oxen. One of their neighbors gave him a pair of rabbits—and you'd never guess how many he had when he got here. He went to the first school in a blacksmith shop. There's plenty of humor in it—and color. There was one night when they danced square dances and took turns standing guard against raiding Indians. . . . Maybe you'll think there's something in it. It's an old man's dream—but even so, I don't want to force anything down your throats."

Johnny leaped lightly down off the stage and took his seat in the front row. The applause was a slower, more thoughtful applause than when Norbett had dangled before them his jolly, gag-line opera.

Melinda stood up. "Now there," she said impartially, "You have the two types of shows. We'll put it to a vote to decide your preference."

And then Norbett Rhodes overplayed his hand. In his consuming anxiety to sell his own idea, he asked for a last word and said vehemently, "Anybody that knows anything at all about theater knows that the whole trend is away from serious stuff. As Melinda says, we've outgrown the usual high-school stuff. We've certainly outgrown any of this historic, covered-wagon tripe." The onimous, stiffening silence should have warned him, but he flung out with sneering superiority, "No matter how you dress it up in hoop-skirts, it's still hokum."

. . . "A salesman's cause is lost as soon as he starts to use sarcasm." . . . Again Beany couldn't keep back a tug of pity. Norbett, Norbett, you goon, she thought helplessly.

"How many would like to put on Norbett's *Romeo and Juliet* opera?" Melinda asked, seeking to keep her voice neutral.

Only a few hands went up. Norbett had been domineering; he had told them what he thought they should have. And, worst of all, he had belittled Johnny Malone.

"How many would like Johnny's early-day Denver idea?"

Even without turning her head Beany felt the rush of hands that made the auditorium like a field of waving wheat. The football fellows even stamped and yelled out, "Covered wagon! Covered wagon!" which was their way of flinging Norbett's sneer back in his face. Johnny hadn't been high-and-mighty. Johnny had shared his fears, his hopes, with an apologetic, "I don't want to force anything down your throats."

Melinda motioned for silence. Her beautiful voice announced, "We will put on *Our City Has Deep Roots*."

Johnny, like his father, Martie Malone, was not the "Hurrah! Hurrah! we've won!" kind. He stood, flanked by Miss Hewlitt and Melinda, looking shaken and sobered. Carlton Buell, his stocky shadow with a crew haircut, was far more beaming and elated than he.

Beany edged her sidewise way out of the second row of

seats slowly. Wasn't anything ever clear-cut black and white? Why couldn't she want her own brother, Johnny, to win out over Norbett Rhodes? Of course she was glad. Of course she was! She was rejoicing that Norbett hadn't got to first base with his *Romeo and Juliet* idea, which would have left the Malones wide open to his jibes.

Johnny took a step toward her. The play was temporarily forgotten for he said, "Hey, Beany! Kay Maffley was telling me in Glee Club about a little stray pooch that followed her home a couple nights ago. She said a car must have run over its foot. She can't keep it at the hotel. And she didn't want to turn it over to the Dumb Friends' League—and so I told her we could take it."

"Johnny, didn't Kay tell you to wear your jacket and cover up that awful shirt?"

Johnny said absently, "Yes, I guess she did. Yes, come to think of it, she did—because that's how we got started talking about dogs, and she told me about this poor little mutt. She said it was so hungry it tried to lick up some old mashed popcorn on the hotel steps. I'd go home with her and get it, but Melinda wants me to stay and talk over the play with her. You can go though, can't you, Beany?"

7

The Winsome Twosome

So, for the first time, a fellow student rode home with Frozen-face in the ice-cream wagon.

Through the drizzly rain beside Kay, Beany ran down the wet Harkness steps, clutching an unwieldy stack of books, notebooks, and her cooking apron which needed washing. Kay opened the door for Beany to get into the back seat; she, herself, scrambled into the front. (But there's plenty of room for three in the front seat, Beany thought.)

Kay introduced Beany to her counterpart behind the wheel with uneasy, almost placating, swiftness. "Faye, this is Beany Malone. She's going to take the dog home with her so you won't have to give it to the Dumb Friends' League. Beany, this is my mother, Faye."

Beany's eyes, under their thick lashes, widened in amazement. Kay was wearing an orchid blouse with a gray suit. Her mother was wearing exactly the same. The only difference was that Kay was without ornament and Faye, her mother, wore a heavy necklace and a jangly charm bracelet. Beany exclaimed, "Your mother! Honest?" and then flusteredly, "How do you do, Mrs. Maffley—only I thought—I thought you were Kay's sister."

"Oh, everyone thinks that," the girl-woman said with a pleased, tinkly laugh. "Everyone calls me Faye—no one ever calls me Mrs. Maffley. Everyone takes me for Kay's twin."

As the car, the color of vanilla ice cream, sped through the rain, Beany's practical mind was doing arithmetic. Kay was sixteen. Her mother must be thirty-six—thirty-four, at least—and she *did* look sixteen, with that pale riot of hair, with that youngish gray suit with patch pockets. No wonder Kay didn't need a girl chum. Beany heard Kay say, "This is a stop street. You should have worn your glasses, Faye." Like one girl to another.

And, like one girl to another, her mother answered, "Oh, those silly glasses! They make me look like that awful old hag in the library at Upton, Utah."

In the lobby of the Park Gate Kay said, "The dog is in the basement, but come up to the apartment, Beany, and I'll give you the salve I got for its foot."

On the eighth floor, Faye, with a tinkle of charm bracelet, unlocked a door. Beany stepped into the Maffley apartment at the Park Gate Apartment Hotel.

It was like a playhouse—a high-priced, detail-perfect playhouse. Beany's first thought was of the havoc a little Martie or their dog, Red, and his wagging plume of tail, would wreak in a place like this. Yes, or even Emerson Worth, going his muttery, nearsighted way. Low tables with fragile figurines, with china vases in the shape of donkeys or doves, out of whose backs ivy grew and trailed. The carpeting was deep piled and ivory colored. A muddy footprint would show as plainly as those footprints in the wet sand on Crusoe's island. A love seat, the chairs, were all pale damask softness—every pillow fluffed into place and unsullied.

"It's just beautiful," Beany breathed.

Faye showed her through the three rooms, happy as a child showing off her playhouse. "See, this is our kitchenette."

"Do you cook here?" Beany asked. Surely those virginal, peach-colored, ruffled curtains had never known stove smoke or steam. Nor had those peach-colored tea towels ever wiped a pan. Beany thought of the big Malone kitchen and the worn spot in the linoleum between stove and sink, of the cavernous oven that always baked a little lopsidedly.

"Just breakfasts—sometimes," Faye said. "We eat in the dining room downstairs. And here's our bedroom."

Beany's "Oh!" was more of a startled, unbelieving grunt.

This bedroom was like a picture out of a Hollywood magazine, showing a star's bedroom. It was like one of the display rooms when their biggest furniture store had shown a "dream house." It was like a stage bedroom.

The curtains, as well as the spreads on the two beds, were of a soft, filmy gray chiffon, sheer and iridescent as a cobweb. Clearly defining the swooped-back fullness and the lavish length, which fell and rested on the floor like a dress train, was a pleated ruffle of scarlet taffeta. The headboards of the beds were rounded and padded with pale gray taffeta. And against them, round red pillows stood out like roses against a gray sky.

"Pearl and lipstick, the decorator called it," Faye said

happily. "He said it was the perfect background for our coloring. Personalized decorating."

No home-covered dressing table here. One wall was completely paneled with mirrors. And against the opposite wall under a glass table top was a multitude of drawers with crystal knobs. There was no spot in the room in which Beany couldn't observe twice that the zipper in her plaid skirt didn't lie as flat as a zipper should. (And she had thought, until now, that she'd done so well putting a zipper in this skirt that had had a buttoned placket when she bought it.) She could even see the knot where she had pieced together the lace in her left saddle shoe.

Faye dropped down in the gray chair before the many-drawered dressing table and, opening a drawer, took out a powder puff and stroked the tip of her nose that the rain might have touched; though it hadn't, really, because she had driven into the garage under the Park Gate Hotel and had ridden thence by elevator to the eighth floor. A gentle, dismissing push and the drawer went nicely shut. No pulling it out farther, and squirming it, and having to lift one knee to shove it back where it belonged so you could push a ruffled skirt back into place.

For the first time Beany felt a discontent with her little room with its blue ceiling (halfway between a robin-egg blue and a madonna blue, the article had said) and the yellow plaid gingham curtains that could pull the sun right out of the sky and into your room. The material in these voluminous pearl-gray curtains hadn't been figured so closely that their ruffle had to be stretched and skimped to reach clear across the bottom. And her gingham curtains *had* shrunk with each washing (though the clerk had insisted the material was preshrunk), so that instead of being floor-length, they were now baseboard length. And the wrist-sized pipe that ran from the radiator to the ceiling *did* show even though she had painted it the same neutral shade as the walls. And the white rug by her bed really was a bathroom rug that looked bumpy and cottony compared to the tufted thick luxury of the gray rug under her feet.

Back in the living room, Kay put a green jar of salve in Beany's hand. "This is what I got for his sore foot. And then I keep it wrapped."

"Okay," Beany promised. "We'll doctor up his foot until it's better."

"I wanted to give him a bath," Kay said regretfully.

Faye said, "Kay, darling, I was afraid you'd be silly and feel badly about parting from that awful little dog, so I brought you this."

She unwrapped and put on the low table in front of Kay a glass dog. "There's your dog. I even named it Muffet for you. Isn't it sweet?"

Kay said tonelessly, "Yes, it's sweet," and turned her face away from the inanimate dog with its pleased, glassy expression.

Faye said to Beany, as though she wanted to hear it again, "So you thought I was Kay's sister? Do you remember the southern colonel, Kay dear, who always referred to us as the winsome twosome? Kay and I have always been chums. We have all our good times together."

Beany shifted in the soft depths of the chair. I wonder what the secret is. Why, she looks younger—yes, and happier—than Elizabeth, and Elizabeth is only twenty-two. Beany *had* to ask it, "But I don't see how you can stay so young, Mrs. Maffley—I mean Faye."

Fay said archly, "Shall I tell her, Kay?"

"Yes, tell her," Kay said.

Faye's gay laugh rippled out. "It isn't really a philos-ophy—philosophy sounds so heavy. I just don't let myself worry. Not ever. I learned a long time ago never to put my-self in a position that might turn out unpleasantly."

Beany listened, almost startled. Then she, Beany, was right. For here was a woman who had kept herself a girl by believing that. Here was Faye, the living embodiment of "don't stick your neck out." Here was proof that the Malone way was wrong.

Beany sat forward on the turquoise chair. "That's what I think, too. But my family— Well, supposing an old man— he's the one Johnny was talking about, Kay—supposing he came wandering into your house, looking so pitiful—what would you do, Faye? You see he has a perfectly awful room—and he forgets to eat—"

Faye said smoothly, "But there are institutions for taking care of just such helpless people. You were foolish not to send him to one."

Beany sank back in the chair. This seemed such a ha-ven—such an untouched, untroubled, and ruffled haven; such a well-locked and hermetically sealed haven, eight floors up from the dreary problems and worries of everyday living.

Kay said bluntly, "I'll go with you to get the dog. It's raining harder, Faye. Couldn't you drive her home—be-cause the dog is lame?"

Faye said gaily, "But we've got to hurry to our dancing class, Kay. You haven't even time to go down to the base-ment with her." And to Beany, "We take dancing lessons twice a week. I made Kay a new costume to wear for Interpretive dancing. It's called Dance of the Hours, and Kay and I are both Dawn."

She slid back the door of a closet and brought out a pink chiffon dress, each flounce edged in black velvet. Beany looked at it enviously; it was soft and frothy as pink soda water. Faye held it up to Kay's slim figure. "And when we wear these dresses, we'll wear our hair like this—" She freed one hand and swooped Kay's cascade of light, shimmering hair back from her face, "—and put a velvet band around with a bow at the back."

There was to Beany something vaguely familiar about Faye's delight in Kay's hair. Why, it was the gesture of a girl fixing her doll's hair to match a new costume; a doll with real live hair.

Beany picked up her stack of books and her cooking apron and went to the basement with the Park Gate janitor for the dog. The dog came limping as the janitor called it. He was a small dog with a sad, buffeted face and a bandaged foot. An apologetic black-and-white dog with some claim—though very little—to wire-haired ancestry. One eye looked out of a black patch—like a vanquished prize fighter.

It does need a bath, Beany realized, as she coaxed it, "Come on, mutt, if you don't wriggle, I'll carry you under my coat. There now," she soothed its whimpering, "I'll be careful of your sore foot."

Beany was standing in the lobby by the revolving door, wondering just how to manage with a squirmy weight of dog under one arm and her books and the wadded-up cooking apron under the other, and thinking of the wet walk through the park and the rain, when a sarcastic voice said, "*Miss* Malone, I believe! And what a lovely evening you've chosen to take your dog for an airing."

It was Norbett Rhodes. Just once, Beany thought, just once, I'd like to bump into Norbett when I'm wearing—well, something like that dawn-pink creation Faye just showed me. But here I am, like an overloaded burro!

She said shortly, "It's Kay Maffley's dog. Only the hotel wouldn't let her keep it, so I—"

"The hotel? You mean that tinseled blond mother of hers wouldn't? How do I know? Because there are two dogs on our floor that I fall over in the corridor twice a day. Well, Miss Samaritan, I'd be most happy to give you a lift home. Only as you know—as well as every other reader of the *Call* —my car is temporarily not at my disposal."

"I can walk," she said coldly.

The dog squirmed so unduly in her arms that her books and the mussed white apron slithered out of her arms onto the floor. As she tried to grab at them, the jar of salve fell out of her coat pocket and rolled partway across the lobby.

Norbett, with a sardonic smile, retrieved them all for her; those awful straps on the cooking apron kept dangling as he put it on top of her books. He dropped the jar of salve into her pocket. "You'll have a nice, wet walk home. Why couldn't you call Johnny up and have him come and get you in *his* car? *His* car would never be impounded. Or is the genius too busy working on the Great American Play?"

Anger flared hotly through her. Anger at Johnny for getting her into this predicament, but greater anger at Norbett who was smacking his lips over his sneers.

"Of course his car wouldn't be impounded. Because he wouldn't be dumb enough to drive it without a brake and light sticker," she flung at him. "He's waiting to get one. Otherwise I would phone him to come and pick me up. I imagine he's home now, though he was to stay and talk over *his* play with Melinda."

"The unbeatable Malones!" he jeered. "The mighty Malones! Did I laugh like crazy at Johnny asking me if I'd handle the lighting for that Last-Stand-of-the-Buffalo thing he's putting on! I wouldn't touch it."

"It was a waste of time, his asking you," Beany said, her voice thick with fury. "I could have told him that. I could have told him you wanted another grudge to carry around and keep yourself thin carrying it." She thought for one frightening moment she was going to cry—and that made her so furious that she fumbled in her mind for one last telling jab. "You wouldn't feel right if you didn't have an excuse for hating the Malones."

She expected an answer couched in fury. But surprisingly enough, he said slowly, "I'd hate you whether I had an excuse or not, Beany. Because you're everything that I'm not. You like people—and everyone likes you. You're like that breakfast food ad on the radio—you're strengthened from inside."

That caught Beany off guard. She was about to falter, "I'm sorry there weren't more hands up on your play— even if you were doing it to rub Malone noses in the dirt—"

But just then a middle-aged man came toward Norbett. A nervous-eyed man with sharp lines about his sharp eyes. Norbett said mockingly, "Here comes my uncle, Beany. I'm sure he'd be happy to meet Martie Malone's daughter."

On that Beany, books, apron with dangling straps, salve, and dog, bolted through the revolving door.

The park, through which Beany walked, was all splashy wetness underfoot, all dripping wetness overhead. Once

she eased the dog out of her aching arm to see if he wouldn't
follow her. He would. But his limp was so pitiful that Beany
picked him up again, even though it meant washing her
pink sweater that night and sponging off her reversible.

She wouldn't think of Norbett Rhodes. . . . Maybe
Mrs. No-complaint had left a casserole of Swiss steak in the
oven. . . . Why wasn't Kay happier with such a wonderful
mother? . . . If only Mary Fred had made enough head-
way on the Nitrogen Family to please the ironclad old
Baggy! . . . If it wasn't for little Martie—yes, and Red
and old Emerson Worth—they could have a lot of figurines
and white china vases sitting around. . . . Would old
Emerson be the alert and dynamic Emerson Worth of his
build-a-city days, or just a quavery old man, still hunting
that mythical lost spike? . . . That hateful Norbett
Rhodes, daring her to meet his uncle! Don't think about
Norbett.

Red, the usual welcoming committee of one, met Beany
at the gate. . . . Why should Red's coat, whether wet or
dry, always remind her of Norbett's hair? . . . Red didn't
condescend to notice the quivering little stranger under
Beany's arm and coat. His wagging wet-feather tail seemed
to say, "Go in, Beany. I'm waiting for Johnny. Then we'll
come in and decide on whatever that is you've brought
home."

Beany stepped into the front hall. It was dusk, that mon-
grel time between daylight and dark, that let-down time
when the day is ended and evening's lights and evening's
bustle have not yet started. The house seemed gloomily
silent—well, almost silent. Emerson Worth was there. They
had two ways of knowing when Emerson was about. When
he was awake he blew his nose with staccato gusts—like

shots from a gun; when he was asleep, his old man's snores vibrated with low, tired-machinery rhythm through the house. Beany stood in the dim hallway and placed his whereabouts. He was sleeping on the couch in the living room.

A queer resentment tugged at her. No one would go stretching out, any time he felt the need, on Faye's oyster-white brocade couch. Beany spilled her armload of books onto the stairs and, still holding the armload of dog who was worriedly licking her chin now, stood in the living-room door.

Something was lacking. Always before, when she came in the house reached loving, durable arms around her. But now, under the influence of all that "prettiness" in Faye's apartment, something in her was standing off, saying critically, "But they're such unpretty, such shabby arms."

Always before the big living room, which took two large rugs to cover, held warm tag-ends of memory for her. Not conscious or catalogued memories, just dim reminders that were in the marrow of her bones.

In that hardy, red-leather chair, which matched the red leather on the window seat and picked up the shades of red in books in the wide, open book shelves, so many guests of Martie Malone's had relaxed—prize fighters, opera singers, swimming champions, the missonary priest from India. Father called the couch where Emerson now rested, with its slip cover that went into Mrs. No-complaint's washing machine when its blue background became gray, the "Convalescent Camp." On it he always deposited any of the children after their parting from tonsils. Toward it Father had made his first shaky trip after his bout with pneumonia.

In front of the fireplace the four Malone stockings had dangled limply on Christmas eve, only to become miraculously knobby and weighted by Christmas morning. Once Elizabeth, coming in chilled from skating, had stood so close to the fire that she had burned the hem of her skirt. There was one loose brick at the side where Beany, at ten, had hidden a birthday locket, just *in case* thieves broke in.

But so many pieces in their living room weren't selected. They just *came*. The white bear rug which some explorer friend of Father's had sent from Alaska. (Years ago Johnny used to wrap himself in it and rush growling at Beany. No wonder all but one of its teeth were gone, and the ears were worn nubs of metal.) The wrought-iron candelabrum Johnny had made in Junior High metal shop for mother. How beaming and radiant she had been when she had fitted white candles in it. "We'll put it under the Sistine Madonna," she had said. But now the candles leaned in different, unsymmetric directions. And the pictures! They hadn't been chosen to carry out a color scheme. Mary Fred had put up a picture of her black horse, Mr. Chips, with the white spot in his forehead that Mary Fred said was a star that fell. The oil painting over the bookcase was of a winding, aspen-bordered mountain road. Mother and Father always said they had taken that very road on their honeymoon.

Personalized decoration! Just in the Malone helter-skelter way, Beany thought dissatisfiedly. Faye would laugh merrily at such a room—at such a house.

Beany heard Johnny slam the side door, tramp wetly to the kitchen. Beany joined him there. Red had come in with him. I'd like to shake myself the way Red does, Beany thought ruefully, as she dodged the spray from him.

"There's your protégé," she said to Johnny and eased the bundle of dog out of her arms.

Johnny hunkered down to pat his damp head. "Welcome to Malone Manor," Johnny said. Red pushed up inquiringly and Johnny said formally, "Red, meet our new guest. Now don't act snobbish—like Mrs. Socially-prominent interviewing a cleaning woman. Remember Rosie O'Grady and the colonel's lady are sisters under the skin. By gosh, Beany, if she hasn't got a name, we'll call her Rosie O'Grady."

"Rosie?" Beany repeated, startled.

Johnny was rummaging in the closet for his oldest pair of corduroys to make her a bed, while Beany sorted through the icebox to find a saucer of stew for her. As she started to put it before Rosie's hungrily sniffing nose, Johnny reproached her, "Beany, we should warm it for her—considering her delicate condition."

"I don't believe it. Kay called her *him*. She didn't know it was a lady dog."

"I have a hunch Kay's mother did," Johnny said succinctly, stirring the stew in a pan over the gas flame.

"Johnny, why did you go sticking your neck out and taking on this Rosie-dog? We'll be so crazy about the pups—but we can't keep them all. Faye is right, we just oughtn't to get ourselves in situations that will prove unpleasant." She thought of the lovely glass dog which Faye had set on the low table. You couldn't get involved with a glass dog. Beany added wistfully, "They've got the prettiest rooms I've ever, ever seen. And Kay's mother is so beautiful—and so young. That's Kay's mother, Johnny, that comes to school after Kay. Only they're just like girl chums. Faye and Kay. A southern colonel always called them the winsome twosome."

"Sounds like a gruesome twosome to me," Johnny said with unexpected malice.

Beany took off her wet shoes and her soaking socks. "Johnny, go on upstairs and change your shoes—and bring down my wool snuggies—" Beany was opening the oven door with hungry expectancy. The oven was blackly, bleakly empty. Beany asked, "Didn't Mrs. No-complaint leave us anything for dinner?"

Johnny indicated a folded sheet that could have come from Mary Fred's chem notebook. "Mrs. No-complaint left us a little *billet doux* which I have just scanned. Mrs. No-complaint is no longer in the half-a-day employment of the Malones. With her seventeen years of satisfactory service behind her, she refuses to work any place where an old man follows her around and accuses her of stealing a silver spike."

You see, Beany thought wetly, hungrily, drearily, that's just what comes of sticking your neck out. If we hadn't taken in poor old Emerson Worth we wouldn't be stranded like this. We'd come home to Swiss steak in the oven and maybe a pie on the drainboard. And now I'll have to wash and iron my cooking apron myself. She said morosely, "Don't act so blithe, Johnny. You know what the want ads are in the paper these days. A two-foot-long list under 'Help Wanted' and not a single one under 'Situations Wanted.'"

"Look at that empty saucer, Beany. That stew was just *hors d'oeuvre* for Rosie O'Grady. . . . Well, we could put an ad in, 'Wanted half a housekeeper who wouldn't mind being accused of stealing a nonexistent silver spike.'"

"And who wouldn't mind a little boy eating up the candle holders—or an expectant mother, named Rosie O'Grady, with a sore foot," supplemented Beany.

"Or an oven that bakes a little lopsided," Johnny added, remembering his Lady Eleanor cake.

8

Beany to the Rescue

"Mary Fred, Lila told me—I saw her at the store just now when I got the hamburger—that you are going to be chosen freshman escort for the Homecoming queen."

Beany had come hurrying in to the kitchen. She went on, as she snapped the string off her flat soft package in butcher's paper, as she dumped the solid lump of ground meat in the black skillet and broke it apart with a fork, "Lila said that because Elizabeth was an escort when she was a freshman and tradition was strong on the campus— and because you're so popular yourself that the Delts were going to back you— Gosh, Mary Fred, why didn't you tell me?"

Beany had interrupted Mary Fred's droning of "4 $FeSo_4$ plus 2 H_2O plus O_2 equals— Murder, he says!—what does it equal?" Mary Fred looked up from her chem book and answered with nervous testiness, "Why didn't I tell you? Because I'm scared to mention it. Because there's this little matter of chem credits between my being a freshman, my being a pledge, my being chosen freshman escort." Mary Fred's blue eyes took on the haunted anxiety that Beany found so troubling.

Beany backed away from the sputtering hamburger. She ducked her head under the neck straps of a blue cellophane apron which turned her coral sweater to lavender. The spaghetti had bubbled to doneness while she had scurried to the store for the meat. As yet Mrs. No-complaint Adams' capable and querulous self had not been replaced. Beany dropped on one knee in front of the oven and scraped out a flat cinder made from a berry pie spilling over.

Half of the round kitchen table was covered with Mary Fred's notebooks and papers. One of her hands had absorbedly clawed a curl out of her soft pompadour and it stood out like a question mark above her anxious face.

It was Monday, the second day of November, and a light sleet snicked at the window like a whisper of warning, "November is here. And the big Varsity Homecoming is close at hand."

From the time school opened in mid-September, all the activities on the campus were just a rising crescendo to the grand climax of Homecoming. For Homecoming, the Varsity football team played their toughest rival. For Homecoming, banners waved from floats and on every campus building and stadium, "Welcome Old Grads." The most popular senior girl would be chosen as Homecoming Queen. One girl from each class would be chosen for her four escorts to ride with her on the loveliest float in the parade, to share with her the glamorous ceremonies at the Homecoming dance.

Beany remembered back to when Elizabeth had been

freshman escort. Photographer's flash bulbs flickering like lightning. Flowers—and more flowers—arriving: flowers from the Delts, from would-be suitors. The telephone's constant ringing. Elizabeth, in pink-cheeked excitement, rushing to breakfast at the Delt house and then home to dress in her escort finery for the parade. The Delt buffet supper wedged between the parade and the big Homecoming dance. Elizabeth choosing corsages to wear to receptions for old grads.

And to have chem formulas barring Mary Fred's way to campus heaven! For by Homecoming, either the sorority rushees were pledged—or were dropped. To have Homecoming looming ahead as a tragic milepost when it could be such a joyous one!

Beany saved out a spoonful of hamburger for Rosie O'Grady, whose beseeching eyes had followed her every move. She slid the casserole of spaghetti, hamburger, and tomatoes into the oven. "Look, Mary Fred," Beany said on the slam of the oven door, "why don't you ask Ander to help you get your Nitrogen and Silicon families straightened out? He's had a lot of chem on account of his taking pre-med."

"It's the Iron family now," Mary Fred sighed, "and, lastly, our dear old Gold and Platinum family. Only, thank heaven, gold and platinum are too ritzy to have as big a family as Nitrogen. . . . Yes, Ander could help—but I just haven't the heart to pester him with my worries. He didn't get back from the war, you know, until the first quarter was almost ended. He's having it pretty thick himself. At night when I stagger to bed, I can see him burning his own midnight oil—or rather, his aunt's electricity."

Ander Erhart was the nephew of Mrs. Socially-prominent

Adams in the white-pillared colonial house next door. Mary Fred had met him her junior year at Harkness when Ander came down from a Wyoming ranch to take premedic. "Mary Fred's horse romance," Johnny always referred to it. For Mary Fred had impulsively brought home the limping black horse, Mr. Chips, and Ander had helped her cure the strained tendon that had made Mr. Chips lame.

Ander had left school, after a few months, to enlist. All the time Ander was overseas Mary Fred had sent him homemade cookies and V-mail letters. And now Ander was back at the university, starting his freshman year of premedic over. Ander was a full-fledged freshman, whereas Mary Fred, as she said, was just a dangling participle because of those missing chem credits left over from high school.

So now, with the sleet whispering at the window, Mary Fred said soberly, "You know, Beany, chem isn't the dreary fog it was. It's all in concentrating on it. But the time is so short—all at once the whole campus is turning itself inside out for Homecoming." A shivery tremor went through her. She pulled her tweed suit jacket closer over her white blouse. "It wouldn't be so bad—though it'd be bad enough—if it wasn't for Lila. But you know how it is with Lila."

Everyone knew how it was with Lila. She had been Mary Fred's shadow ever since their kindergarten days. Lila was shy and gentle and utterly dependent on what Johnny called Mary Fred's bubble and bounce. There was nothing outstanding about Lila, but because it was always "Mary Fred and Lila," the Delts had tacitly included her when they rushed Mary Fred. Lila would either bubble and bounce with Mary Fred—or flop with her.

Mary Fred was musing aloud: "This coming Friday

evening the chem lab will be open. Professor Baggy will be there, grading notebooks. If I could have just one free, unmolested evening without Norbett Rhodes being there, I believe I could dig in like a gopher and finish up all my formulas."

Beany said defensively, "How does Norbett keep you from getting your chem?"

"Oh, just every way!" Mary Fred said drivenly. "He has the work table next to mine, and he clatters around, making belittling remarks just to get under Baggy's skin. And you know what contempt does to Baggy. Baggy thinks chem formulas are as sacred—oh yes, and a lot more important than, the ten commandmants. Old Baggy gets so edgy—and he classes me with Norbett as an uppity senior or, even worse, a college freshman looking down my nose at high-school chem. And he gets positively sadistic. And that isn't all Norbett does," Mary Fred added viciously. "He whistles under his breath. It's always the same tune—"

Mary Fred imitated Norbett's whistling of "Tura, lura, lura—" "But he never finishes it, Beany. If he'd only finish it. I keep waiting for the windup line, but no, he stops. It's like waiting for the second shoe to fall. I don't even mind his mixing things that are always sizzling over—and once something he mixed exploded. But I'd rather be blown through the skylight than to have him bedeviling me with his whistling." She added longingly, "If there was only *some way* to keep Norbett out of chem lab Friday night so I could wind up all this nightmarish business!"

Beany said, "Friday night is the night Miss Hewlitt is entertaining the new soph members of her Lit Society." Even as she said it—before she was even aware of a thought being born—her heart began a fluttery thump-thump. . . .

Now look out, Beany, she reminded herself. Remember that Norbett is nipping at Mary Fred's heels because he likes *her*. Remember how hateful he was about the play; it wasn't his fault that he didn't get away with that *Romeo and Juliet* idea, just so he could get laughs at the Malones' expense. . . .

But it wouldn't hurt, she argued back, to ask him to go to Miss Hewlitt's Get-acquainted. Because Miss Hewlitt told the girls to bring any escorts they wanted. And you'd be doing it for Mary Fred. You promised Father you'd look after the family.

Beany tried to make her voice casual. "Maybe I could ask Norbett to go—with me—" her voice squeaked thinly, "to the Lit party at Miss Hewlitt's house. Norbett—sits next to me in typing—and lots of times I help him with his spelling." And once, she was remembering, he had asked her to go with him to a football game.

"Oh gosh, Beany! Greater love hath no man than to take Norbett out of the chem lab. Talk about a burnt offering! But could you endure his lousy disposition for a whole evening?"

Beany bent her head to adjust the oven regulator. She couldn't admit to Mary Fred—she couldn't even admit it to herself. It wouldn't be *enduring* Norbett!

Mentally Beany did much rehearsing of a casual approach to asking Norbett to go to the Lit party with her. . . . "Norbett, Miss Hewlitt is gathering the flock— the Lit Society means so much to her—and so I wondered if maybe you—" No, maybe she could go at it from another angle, "Do you suppose you could get a story for your *Tribune* out of the Lit Meeting at Miss Hewlitt's?" . . .

But both Tuesday's and Wednesday's fifth-hour typing

went by. Both days Norbett came in, hurriedly pounded
out a page or two, and left. She'd have to ask him Thursday.
Because some Fridays Norbett covered high-school games
for his paper and wasn't there.

On Thursday Beany went in to typing class resolutely.
She'd start talking casually about their Drill Exercise and
then—

But it didn't work out that way. Miss Meigs had a
student teacher observing and Miss Meigs wanted the class
to make a businesslike impression. She said crisply, "Now,
students, you are here to become efficient in typing. Let
us not waste time visiting."

Let us not waste time! Desperately, Beany put a sheet
of paper in her machine and wrote,

> Beany Malone requests the pleasure of Norbett
> Rhodes' company to Miss Hewlitt's get-acquainted for
> the Lit Society tomorrow night.

She slid the paper across the small space between her
typewriter and Norbett's.

He read it, put the paper in his machine, and whisked
out an answer,

> Norbett Rhodes accepts with pleasure. Sounds like
> a fine, large evening. Cider and popcorn and oh-ing
> and ah-ing over Miss Hewlitt's dolls. I've been there be-
> fore.

Beany snickered stealthily over that. The gray-haired,
round-shouldered Lit teacher, who had taught Shakespeare
to two generations of Harkness pupils, was a collector of
dolls. One end of the big living room in her bungalow was
taken over by them.

"An old maid's children," she always belittled her hobby, even as she observed closely whether her visitor showed interest in any or all of the dolls from Argentina, from China, from Hungary. Hundred-year-old dolls, a ballet dancer doll, a doll in Scottish kilts. One doll whose head was a red-cheeked apple. It was said at Harkness that once she had passed her dullest pupil because he had commented on the homespun petticoat on the Irish doll.

Beany wrote a further message to Norbett,

Maybe you could write up the meeting for the *Tribune* so it wouldn't be an entirely wasted evening for you.

With a sardonic smile on his face he typed out some would-be *Tribune* headlines:

PORTUGUESE PRINCESS SOCKS THE HIGHLAND LADDIE

HUNGARIAN GYPSY TAKES A BITE OUT OF APPLE LADY

With a still more sardonic smile, he added,

Norbett Rhodes regrets exceedingly that he cannot call for Beany Malone in his car, but, owing to fate or, should I remind you, a certain columnist, that is impossible.

Beany didn't even mind that barbed shot. Norbett Rhodes had accepted with pleasure!

What should Beany Malone wear to the party to which Norbett Rhodes would escort her? She had gone to innumerable school affairs with Carlton Buell but never had she known this consuming anxiety to look just right.

She came home from school that day and went right to the clothes closet in her room. Not that she needed to stand there and shove back and forth the garments that hung on coat hangers on the broom-handle rod in her closet. She knew every one by heart, but there was a small hope that she'd discover *something* she might have forgotten.

Not any of her sweaters and skirts. A get-acquainted party was a notch above sweaters and skirts. Not too dressy a dress, either. This peasant blouse that Father had sent from Hawaii and which she wore with a gathered skirt? No. A dark-haired senorita type might look like a fiesta dancer in it, but Beany—so Carlton Buell said—looked like a peasant milkmaid. Slowly she shoved past her one long dress that she had worn at the "Continuation" exercises when she left Junior High. Of course it would never do to wear a yellow taffeta, with tiny blue flowers in it and blue ribbon bows along the flounce, to a Lit party, but she felt its soft swish under the faded housecoat that covered and protected it, and she thought fleetingly of how nice it would be to wear it to a dance with Norbett. . . . This velveteen suit that she had thought the last word six months ago? Oh, now! It looked so woefully junior high; and besides, the skirt was the kind you had to keep tugging over your knees.

Then the question was solved. Mary Fred came bolting into her room with the question, "Did you get Norbett to go? So he won't be prodding Baggy and me?" (as though Norbett were an intractable bull that had to be got out of a pasture) and Beany said, "Yes—yes, I did. But I just don't know what to wear."

Mary Fred said generously, "You can wear anything I've got, as long as you're taking my Nemesis out of chem. Come on in our room."

Mary Fred sorted through her closet. "Look, lamb, how about this navy-blue number with the tricky collar and cuffs? The cuffs open out like a fan, in case you get hot and bothered." Beany hesitated, and Mary Fred yanked out another hanger. "I tell you;—this white wool with the wide suede belt. Try it on."

She helped Beany peel her sweater off over her out-stretched arms and snatched up the skirt Beany stepped out of. She dropped the soft, white wool dress over Beany's head and pulled the front fullness in place. "Oh my dear," Mary Fred said, imitating a clerk's suave and affected voice, "that dress does something for you! It has such a casual charm—don't you know?—and there's nothing so flattering to a lovely skin like yours as white. We're selling dresses like this to the girls who are wintering in Miami. Just see how the blue belt brings out the blue in your eyes. Oh my dear, it's *your* dress! . . . Look, Elizabeth, look at our baby sister. Doesn't she look like an ad in *Charm?*"

Elizabeth said, "You'll need heels with it, honey. Gee, I think my blue pumps will match that blue. Here, slip them on. They okay?"

"Oh yes," Beany said. They were a little tight, but what were tight pumps when they matched the blue belt that matched your eyes?

Elizabeth leaned over and kissed Beany's flushed cheek. "Beany, you look so sweet—and so just on the edge of some-thing. You're growing up."

"And you can wear my new Chesterfield," Mary Fred went on. "You'll be a knockout. Too bad to waste all that on old sourpuss Norbett."

Beany lowered her eyes. For her heart was thumping excitedly—and not with any thought of "wasting" all this on Norbett.

And so the next evening, while Mary Fred Malone worked in the chem lab without benefit of an unfinished whistled tune, Beany Malone added Mary Fred's Chesterfield to the pyramid of wraps on the bed in Miss Hewlitt's front bedroom, while Norbett added his leather coat to the pyramid of other leather coats in the back bedroom.

Norbett had called for Beany—only not quite in the accepted manner. Norbett arranged that he and Beany could double-date with a friend of his who had a car. So while Beany waited flutteringly for Norbett to sound their knocker, or for the car, in which they would ride, to come into their driveway and to the front door, Norbett's friend came and said, "Hey, Beany—we've been honking and honking for you. We're out in front. Come on." (Norbett must have sent him in. Oh dear, all this "never darken your door" stuff between the Malones and the Rhodeses!)

Norbett was his nicest self at the party. Not show-off Norbett. Not enemy-of-mankind Norbett. He gave interested, flattering attention to the doll collection, even commenting on the miniature shells in the necklace of the Hawaiian one. But he didn't comment about the blue belt making Beany's eyes bluer.

Miss Hewlitt's friendship for the Malone family was more than that of the Lit teacher at Harkness High. When the English children, Jock and Lorna, made their home with her because the house of her caretaker, the children's great-uncle Charley, was too small, it was the Malones she was always turning to. "Your house draws them like a magnet," she would always say when she came after them....And

Beany's generous heart *had* drawn them like a magnet.
Until that day when they had left so abruptly, so heart-
lessly—and Beany had resolved to demagnetize her
heart. . . .

But the friendship between Miss Hewlitt and the Malones
went farther back than that. She had taught Martie Malone.
When Martie had sought out Emerson Worth for his first
newspaper job he was carrying a folded letter of recom-
mendation from Miss Hewlitt. Miss Hewlitt had never
missed reading a Martie Malone column. "Martie Malone,"
she told her classes, "is like Lincoln—with malice toward
none."

And now Johnny was her pet, her protégé. She mothered
the genius in Johnny, mothered the careless boy in him.
"That's a wonderful curtain line you have—Johnny Malone, your feet are sopping. Go put them on the radiator.
Now, let's see how you handled that first Christmas in
Denver." Her whole heart was in Johnny's play, in Johnny's
paying tribute to the man, Emerson Worth—pioneer
newspaperman. For she, too, was fearful lest the tribute
come too late.

So, quite naturally, at the Lit party, Miss Hewlitt sig-
naled to Beany to help her serve the cider. As Beany arranged the mugs on trays, Miss Hewlitt said, "I was
certainly surprised to see Norbett Rhodes come with you."

Beany pushed down the impulsive honesty that would
have admitted, "I wanted him." She said instead, "I asked
him so he couldn't be working in chem lab—so he couldn't
heckle Mary Fred."

That mollified Miss Hewlitt. "I could certainly have
shaken Norbett that day in auditorium when he tried to
belittle Johnny's dramatizing Emerson Worth's story. And

afterward, when Johnny asked him if he'd handle the lighting, Norbett was downright hateful. 'Maybe you'd like me to tear newspapers up in little bits and sift it down for snow—you couldn't have a covered wagon epic without a snowstorm.' " Miss Hewlitt's imitating of Norbett's tone had the usual overdose of contempt and acid which people always inject into their repeating of speeches that have angered them. " 'Well thanks, Malone,' Norbett said, 'but you can slice your bologna any way you like it. Only don't count me in.' "

"I know," Beany said unhappily.

Miss Hewlitt sighed. "I've often had to remind myself what I learned in a psychology course. That the biggest showoffs, like Norbett, are the ones who aren't sure of themselves."

"But why isn't he?" Beany asked. She shifted her weight off Elizabeth's left pump which pinched more than the right.

"He's never felt wanted. His parents are dead and his aunt and uncle, who raised him, are the selfish, begrudging kind. A friend of mine lives at the Park Gate and she tells me that they have made life miserable for him over that traffic jam he got in. Not because of any ethical or moral issue, mind you, but because it put his traffic-manager uncle in a bad spot."

"Oh," Beany said, as the cider gurgled out of the jug into the mugs.

"Look out for your white dress, Beany! Now how many is that? . . . Yes, this friend of mine says that the uncle as good as told Norbett that he'd have to redeem himself some way—meaning, of course, to get something on you Ma-lones."

"Norbett even admits it. That he's just living for the day when he can rub any or all of our noses in the dirt."

"I think the boy is lonely and insecure. I've often thought the real Norbett under his strut is all right," Miss Hewlitt said. After all, he had noticed the shell necklace on her Hawaiian doll!

Beany and Norbett, and Norbett's friend and the friend's girl friend all stopped at Downey's Drug on the way home for a hot bowl of chile. Surely Beany's shivers weren't from the cold, when she was wearing Mary Fred's coat with the sheepskin lining! Surely bowls of sepia-colored chile had never had such a rare and wondrous fragrance! Surely Norbett had noticed that the blue bodice-shaped belt made her eyes bluer!

They decided to top off the chile with pie. Beany took blueberry. And Norbett sang out lustily, "I dream of Beany with the light blue teeth—"

The Rhodes-Malone feud seemed to shrink farther and farther into the background. Maybe Norbett's liking for Mary Fred had cooled now that he knew she was Ander Erhart's near-steady. While the others loitered over the magazine rack, thumbing through movie magazines, Beany slipped back and stealthily bought the freckle cream.

She would use it tonight.

As Beany opened their front door Johnny was going up the stairs, carrying a too-full bowl of something which slopped over as he stopped to look down at her.

Beany took a moment to kick off and pick up the hurting pumps. She sniffed appraisingly. "Something smells scorched. What did you burn?"

"What did I burn? Listen at her. Maybe a little milk

boiled over while I was hunting for the electric heat pad."

"The electric heat pad! Is Emerson sick?"

"No, Madam-Owsell, Emerson and I have just put in a very scurrying evening of it."

"What are you taking bread-and-milk upstairs for?"

"It's dog niblets and milk. And it is for the new mother, who needs something warming to keep up her strength."

"Rosie? Honest, Johnny? How many?"

"Four."

"What color?"

"Assorted."

"But aren't they down in the basement?"

"The basement is no place for the newborn. There's too much smell of gas from the hot-water heater. Rosie— Mrs. O'Grady, I should say—is in your room in that se- cluded corner between your bed and the wall. I took her to my room, but when I started typing, it disturbed them. I didn't dare put them where little Martie could manhandle them. But Rosie likes your room."

"I want to see what they look like."

"I don't see how you can tonight. I've got the heat pad attached to your light. You can undress in the dark tonight, can't you? I don't think you ought to turn on a light any- way—it might make Rosie nervous."

Wouldn't you know it, Beany thought—oh, wouldn't you know! The one night I wanted to read directions and smear the freckle cream on, I'm supposed to tread softly in the dark so as not to disturb Rosie and the new family. I knew we were sticking our necks out when we brought her home. You can't help loving little pups that you hear whimpering by your bed. Oh dear—here we've got the problem-Rosie while Kay has an unproblem glass dog.

She threw herself crosswise on her bed, reached a wary hand down. If Rosie's bed seemed warm, she would detach the heat pad and put on her light. A soft, licking tongue met her fingers—a grateful, beseeching, loving tongue. Beany's fingers patted the head as she crooned, "There now, Rosie—there now. We'll take care of you and your babies." . . . She could put the freckle cream on in the bathroom. . . .

9

Smashing Traditions

For over a week the penny postals that winged their way from Barberry street to Martie Malone in a small Arizona town were written by joyous hands.

Johnny's, of course, told about Rosie's pups. (Father had already been made intimately acquainted with Rosie, via postals.) "Two black-and-white ones, bearing marked resemblance to their mother. And one black, and one brown, leaving some doubt as to the color of the father." Johnny wrote, too, that the play was progressing with only now and then a buffalo wallow to cross. And that Emerson hadn't found the lost silver spike as yet.

Elizabeth couldn't get all of her news on a postal. She wrote a letter. For at last—at long last, Elizabeth's telephone call had come through. At last an impersonal operator's voice had said, "I have a telegram from San Francisco for Mrs. Donald McCallin—"

"This is she," Elizabeth had breathed out in hope and—fear.

"The telegram is signed, Don. 'Just landed. Will call you as soon as possible. All my love, Don.' Would you care to send an answer?"

"Later," Elizabeth had choked, "later—"

Elizabeth drew them all into her happiness. As though she encircled them all with her arms and said, "Share my happiness with me, even as you shared my worry." . . . "Mary Fred, should I get a new suit to meet Don in, or should I have my old fur coat relined?" . . . "What do you think, Emerson, should we cut off little Martie's curls or should we leave them on till Don gets home?" . . . "If we ordered fries now, Beany, they'd keep till Don gets home, wouldn't they? Let's have fried chicken and ice cream for him when he comes home!" (But not pink ice cream, Beany vowed.) . . . "Johnny, get the brake and light sticker on your car, so we can meet Don's train." . . .

"Do you suppose he'll get back in time for Homecoming?" Beany asked. Plans had already started yeasting in Beany's mind. Elizabeth had received a special invitation to be in the receiving line at the reception. "Welcome Old Grads. Welcome G.I.'s." Beany could picture Lieutenant Donald McCallin, broad-shouldered, handsome, a little grim, as befitted a warrior, and with all his service stripes setting off his uniform, standing proudly beside Elizabeth. Oh, Elizabeth, have fun, Beany longed. Show off Don. Dress up and go to the dance. Wear a pink frothy dress like Dawn.

"When he calls," Beany said, "tell him to hurry on home."

"As though I wouldn't," Elizabeth said prayerfully.

Beany hardly knew what to write on her postal. It wouldn't make sense to say, "I'd like to be friends with a girl named Kay, but, for some reason, she doesn't want to be friends with me." Or, "I went to a party with Norbett Rhodes, nephew of N. J. Rhodes, safety manager. He was so nice that night but—nothing came of it."

Was Norbett avoiding her, or was he too busy these days to come to typing class? Norbett took fifth-hour typing merely to improve his speed and accuracy, not for a credit. If Father were only here, she could talk things out with him. She knew a surge of nostalgic longing for his heartening presence. But the young Malones were all in conspiracy not to trouble Father; he must have a few months to get tanned and rested and vigorous.

There wasn't anyone else she could tell about Norbett's coldness. She had mentioned it to Mary Fred and Mary Fred had only laughed. "Hot-and-cold-running Norbett," Mary Fred had dismissed it.

On Monday, a week and two days after the Friday when Beany and Norbett had attended Miss Hewlitt's soiree, Beany was walking home from school. She had started out with friends walking her way, but now she left them and turned up Barberry street alone.

She had hoped Kay would ask her to ride home with her and her mother, Faye. Yesterday Faye—not the younger Kay—had asked her. Faye had asked her to stop for a visit and tea at the Maffley apartments. Such a wonderful tea.

Beany had no way of knowing that it was her open adoration that Faye found so flattering. "We'll have tea," Faye had said, going to her room telephone and calling the hotel kitchen.

A waiter, all servile deference, brought up a silver tea set, and tiny cream puffs, and salted nuts. Faye had changed into a sea-green velvet hostess gown with silver slippers which matched the silver lace pocket on the gown. Faye, like a fairy-tale princess. Faye laughing again about the southern colonel calling them the winsome twosome. She laughed so easily, so merrily. She showed Beany the skating costumes she was making for her and Kay. Pleated plaid skirts and velvet jackets with gray fur at the neck and wrists. "I love to waltz on skates," she said enthusiastically.

"Elizabeth and Don used to waltz on the park lake," Beany said, remembering.

Again, at Beany's prodding, Faye told her philosophy. She even added to it, "Never trouble trouble and trouble won't trouble you." "Some people really go out of their way to do things the hard way," she said, drinking tea and eating the tiny cream puffs with childish relish. "I just can't stand worry, can I, Kay?"

She told about a time when Kay's father had to have an appendicitis operation. But she knew that if she sat and waited there in the dreary, smelly hospital it would only make her sick and what good would it do? "It wouldn't do anyone any good, now would it, Beany?"

"No," Beany said wholeheartedly, "it wouldn't do anyone any good."

Beany walked alone up Barberry street, musing bewilderedly about Kay and her odd aloofness. Kay never once said, "Pile in, Beany, and go home with us." Yet at school Kay reached hungrily toward Beany. Kay couldn't ask enough questions about Mrs. O'Grady's pups. Was the brown one still the roly-poliest? Had they named them yet? No, not yet.

Yesterday, Kay had even come running up the stairs to catch Beany and pant out, "How about *Pierre?* When I was a little girl I read a story about a dog named Pierre that rescued someone in a snowstorm in the Alps. I always wanted a dog named Pierre."

Beany was just turning into their driveway when a book suddenly hit her in that part of the anatomy known as the fanny. It was a chemistry book and Mary Fred was leaping out of Lila's roadster, yelling in glad hysteria. "You can have it, Beany! It's all yours! I never want to see it again. But the notebook I'm keeping to hand down to my grandchildren, like a Congressional medal. Look here, Beany—look!"

On the first page of the black loose-leaf notebook, in red pencil and Baggy's prim hand, was a "B," and under it, "Passing chemistry 12 A."

"You passed, Mary Fred?" Beany breathed in awe.

"With the grace of God and your help in getting Norbett out from under foot. Beany, we've got to celebrate."

Mary Fred fluttered through the house in restless ecstasy. She telephoned Ander Erhart and, when he wasn't there, left word with his aunt that he was to come over the minute he came home. Very important! She wrote a postal to her father, "I am now a full-fledged freshman, *Deo gratias.*"

Ander opened the side door. "I came on a dead lope. What goes?"

"Mary Fred goes out of the chem lab," Mary Fred chirruped. She added, startled, "Ander, you're sopping wet!"

"Listen to my shoes squash." Ander demonstrated with a half-grim, half-amused smile. "The sophs just ducked me in the fountain outside Old Main."

"What for?" Beany asked.

"Oh, just part of that campus cop-and-robber game that I won't play. I've told them and told them that I haven't

time for it. I didn't mind so much when they tossed me in—
let them have their fun, I thought—but when I started to
climb out and one of them thought he'd push me back—
then I really let them have it. I let my fists do my talking
today."

"Why, Ander," Mary Fred laughed, "don't you know
you're breaking hallowed tradition?"

"It's high time it was broken," he said, and now his smile
was entirely grim. "I outgrew that kid stuff even before
I went to war and had to play it real. And so have the other
G.I.'s. We've lost too much time already. A lot of us were
late getting back. We're ready to settle down and plug.
I want to get through medical before I have long gray
whiskers."

There was something "big" about Ander. He was tall,
but not any taller than many other twenty-one-year-olds.
But even when, as now, he wore cords and brogues and was
hatless, you almost saw him in chaps and boots and a wide
Stetson. His eyes had a far-sighted blueness.

Ander called those ironclad rules regarding freshman
and the enforcing of them "calf's play." Freshmen must
wear a little green cap. Freshmen must step aside on the
walk and salute upperclassmen—especially sophomores.
Certain parts of the campus were sacred ground where a
freshman dared not tread.

Ander had been served a summons to appear before
Kangaroo Court for his failure to heed these injunctions.
In Kangaroo Court penalties were meted out; scrubbing the
steps of Old Main with a toothbrush. Carrying a shoe-
shining outfit and shining the shoes of any upperclassman
who desired a shine.

Ander had wadded up the summons the sophomores had

served him and gone his own way. And now the irate sophs
had retaliated by ducking him in the fountain. And Ander
had let his fists do his explaining.

But Ander and Mary Fred thought it was something to
laugh over. Ander and Mary Fred went right on planning
a horseback ride as celebration. They were always delighted
for an excuse to get out to Mary Fred's Mr. Chips and
Ander's Mike, that he had brought down from Wyoming.

"I'll get my clothes changed," Ander was saying, "while
you get into your riding togs, Mary Fred. How about my
getting some steaks and cooking our supper? This nice
weather is too good to last—it's a weather-breeder, so we'd
better take it while we've got it."

"Beany has to be in on it. Wasn't it her fine hand that
put me through chem? Hunt up your jodhpurs, Beany.
We'll ask Carlton for you. Go on, Ander, and change—you
give me the shakes just to look at you."

Elizabeth said to Johnny, "Why don't you go, too? I'll
be here to take care of Emerson. Take an evening off from
your typewriter and the snows of yesteryear."

"I haven't got a girl," Johnny said.

"I know," Beany said. "I'll ask Kay!"

"Do you think she'd like to go—with me?"

Would she indeed, Beany thought. For she had seen Kay
walking out of Glee Club with Johnny. Beany knew that
rapt, enchanted look. It was the same one Elizabeth wore
when she walked beside the broad-shouldered, twinkling-
eyed Donald McCallin. The same Mary Fred had when she
and Ander made fun of each others' saddles. (*Postage
stamp*, Ander called Mary Fred's English model; that
cruising vessel of yours, Mary Fred always flung back at his
heavy western one.) It was the look Beany, herself, had to

guard against when Norbett Rhodes swaggered into typing.

Beany telephoned the Maffley apartment at the Park Gate. "Kay, we're going riding, and how about you going as Johnny's girl?" She could hear Kay's eager breath, "Oh, it'd be heavenly. Wait just a minute—"

In less than a minute a flat voice that was scarcely recognizable as Kay's—the voice of Frozen-face—said, "I'm sorry, but I won't be able to go."

Beany replaced the receiver with a queer, baffled anger. Kay and her airs! Faye, her mother, was all happy, young graciousness.

Carlton Buell was a nice boy to relax with. A nice boy to jog along with while Mary Fred and Ander raced each other to the dam a mile away. A nice boy to eat supper with and say, "Carl, you gave me the littlest piece of steak," and have him answer unperturbedly, "So what? That's all you deserve."

Just nice. No funny little heart-soarings as when Norbett had warbled out, "I dream of Beany with the light blue teeth." When she sat beside Norbett she couldn't think of anything else. But, sitting beside Carlton Buell, her relaxed mind took happy, satisfied inventory of the Malone family. She hadn't done too well at managing Johnny. But then Johnny was like this amiable horse Mary Fred had chosen for her; he went his own preferred gait no matter how Beany slapped the reins.

But she, Beany, the Malone protector, had helped Mary Fred get both her feet in campus heaven. No longer was one foot mired in Harkness' chem lab. And Elizabeth had heard from Don. Beany must somehow see that Elizabeth got her share of fun and gadding-about clothes from now on. Maybe Faye would lend them the skating costume and Beany could help Elizabeth copy it. Elizabeth and Don could waltz to music under the lavender spotlight on the frozen lake at the park. . . . She tried not to take inventory of her own happiness. But why didn't Norbett pay her any attention—either fighting or otherwise?

Ander was looking at the moon with weatherwise eyes. "It's a spilling moon—that means a storm," he said.

And Carlton added, "Yeh—lots of snow in the mountains. Swell skiing. The *Tribune* is sponsoring a ski meet this week."

. . . Why, that was it! Norbett was busy covering the ski meet in the mountains for his paper. . . .

Ander was right about those golden, warm days being a weather-breeder. The next day snowflakes, large and leisurely as wet feathers, came sifting down.

The telephone was ringing that afternoon when Beany, returning late from school, walked through the front door. She held the receiver to her wet, cold ear, noting as she did the paper pushed under the telephone bearing Elizabeth's message, "Have gone up College Boul. to buy a new hat."

The high-pitched, excited voice at the other end of the phone was that of Mrs. Sears, mother of Mary Fred's chum, Lila.

"Who is this? Oh, Beany, is Mary Fred there?"

"No, no one is home yet. Wasn't this the evening the pledges were to talk over trimming the float for the Homecoming parade?"

"Have you seen this evening's *Tribune?*"

"No. I just brought it in."

"Oh, it's a perfectly awful write-up about Ander. First page and screaming headlines. Listen, 'Cowboy G.I. Turns

Maverick. Defies Fifty-year Tradition on Campus. Brings
Down Ire of All Students.' It says he's being reprimanded
by the Campus Pep Club. It says the Student Council will
undoubtedly take action. Beany, you know what that will
mean?"

"No. What?"

"It will finish Mary Fred if she—well, if she keeps on
going with Ander—for, after all, my dear, it is campus
tradition. You can't blame the sororities and frats for out-
lawing these mavericks, as the paper calls them. Oh, I do
hope Mary Fred won't let her foolish loyalty . . . Because
Mary Fred and Lila aren't pledged yet. Oh, it just makes
me sick all over to think . . ."

Beany managed to hang up on another "—just sick all
over. . . ."

Beany, too, was just sick all over as she unfolded the wet
paper and the headlines leaped at her from the pink outer
sheet. But sometimes headlines were worse than the con-
tent. But not this time. One sophomore, it said, was nursing
a bruised jaw, another had an eye bandaged because of
"Cowboy Andy from Wyoming running amok and smash-
ing traditions and jaws at the same time."

No wonder Lila's mother was sick all over. For years it
had angered Mrs. Sears that her daughter was the "whither
thou goest, Mary Fred" kind, but now that she had accepted
it, she wanted to be sure Mary Fred went the right way.

It wasn't fair. Beany had helped Mary Fred get through
the barrier of chem so that the road was clear for Mary
Fred's being pledged, for her being chosen freshman escort. And now this vitriolic, this biased write-up of Ander
Erhart who "went with" Mary Fred.

Beany was the daughter of a newspaperman. "Give the

public both sides," Martie Malone always said. If only Father were here to take up the cudgels in defense of Ander and the other G.I.'s, who had outgrown what Ander termed campus cop-and-robber stuff. If this was one of Emerson's good days, maybe he could. But Emerson wasn't at home. Why, of course, Elizabeth had turned little Martie over to him while she tried on hats. Probably Emerson and the little boy were sitting happily in some picture show.

The power of the Press! . . . What about Norbett Rhodes? He was school reporter for the *Tribune*. He could give the other side. Norbett was enough of a maverick himself so that he wouldn't think tradition was holy. It came—warming and heartening—the picture of Norbett and his opera role in the scarlet-lined blue cape, "I stand for justice, be he prince or beggar."

Yet it was with heart-thudding furtiveness that Beany dialed the Park Gate number, asked for the Rhodes apartment. None of the Malones must know she was calling Norbett Rhodes to ask for help. But Norbett *had* been nice about going to Miss Hewlitt's party.

A woman's voice, bored and irritable, answered, "This is Mrs. Rhodes."

"Is Norbett there?"

"No, he isn't."

"Oh! Do you know where he is? I wonder if he—if he'd be at the *Tribune*."

"He's staying at school to do some make-up work—math or chem, I don't know which." (My goodness, didn't his aunt know that chem was Norbett's Waterloo?)

While Beany hesitated, the woman said curtly, "I told him to be home promptly at six. Because we're having dinner guests this evening."

Beany couldn't say, "Have him call Beany Malone." Not when the name was anathema to the Rhodeses.

She looked desperately at the kitchen clock. Twenty minutes to six! She'd have to hurry to catch Norbett before he left chem lab. She could never make it, trudging through the snow.

But there was Johnny's car sitting out in the garage. Johnny hadn't driven it because he was waiting to get the brakes and lights checked so as to have an up-to-date brake and light sticker on his windshield.

"Those who carry the banner must walk carefully," a voice from memory nudged remindingly at Beany. She argued back, "But I have to catch Norbett at Harkness. I can't go to the home of safety-manager Rhodes, can I, and beg Norbett to turn out a newspaper column to help the Malones?"

She retied her damp wool scarf over her head, still arguing against that reproachful voice. "But it's such a little ways to Harkness in a car—just down the boulevard and through the park. Who's going to know I took the car? Besides it's for Ander's—yes, and Mary Fred's, sake. That's more important than walking carefully when you carry a banner."

She backed the car out of the garage and drove through the heavy snow to Harkness High.

10

The Missing Door Handle

Queer how unnaturally frowning and forbidding an empty school building can be! Beany's feet echoed hollowly as she walked through Harkness' empty, dimly lighted hall and up the steps—the steps which in daytime spilled over with clomping feet. These wide, yawning corridors couldn't be the same ones she had to shove her way through in broad daylight.

The lights were burning brightly in chem lab. Thank goodness, Norbett was still there. He was at his work table in the back of the room, holding a test tube up to the light and studying it with defeated, helpless anger in his eyes.

But this was no time to consider Norbett's moods. Beany went hurrying up to him. She said on an uneven, panting breath, "Norbett, I came here—I want you to do something for—well, for us."

His hazel eyes looked into her troubled, blue-gray ones, with the heavy lashes stuck wetly together, and his held a deep and mocking anger. "I thought I'd done my good deed for the Malones for this year of our Lord. Don't you remember I spent that edifying and inspirational evening with you and the Harkness Literary Lights?"

It was as though some ugly chemical had corroded the nice friendliness of the Norbett who had noticed the seashell necklace on Miss Hewlitt's doll.

He went on mockingly, "Or don't you remember that you lured me into that just so Mary Fred could work here, untroubled, in the chem lab—so she could coddle old Baggy, without my obnoxious presence? And so Hurrah, Hurrah, for Beany Malone helping Mary Fred to pass chem!"

"How did—how did you know?" Beany faltered shakily, ashamedly.

"Because Mary Fred had to crow about it." Every word came out like an angry whiplash. "After all, it was too good to keep. She had to let the whole school in on it, so they could crow, too. And it was so good they had to rub it into me."

. . . That isn't the whole truth, Beany thought, heartsick. But now—oh, now I'd be boiled in oil before I admitted that I wanted to ask you. . .

"And just how could I be of assistance to the dear Malones this time?"

Beany said flatly, "I came to ask you if you'd write up the other side of this Ander Erhart affair. Because whoever wrote this up in the *Tribune* wrote it so mean and vicious— and unfair. I thought you'd be willing to write it up truthfully and give Ander's side—and all the G.I.'s."

"You thought I'd go rushing to the rescue of this noble Ander person that Mary Fred pushed me in the face for?

And just why did you pick me for this signal honor?"

Beany answered desperately, honestly, "I thought you were that kind of a person. I've always thought you were. The first time I ever saw you—don't you remember your lines in the opera? 'I stand for justice, be he prince or beggar.' "

He laughed with disagreeable heartiness. "Holy cats, Beany, I was just spouting a part. If I'd played Brigham Young, you wouldn't expect me to bob up with twenty-two wives or however many the old boy had." She didn't answer, and he fairly hurled his next words at her, "Don't you know who scampered around and turned in that write-up in the *Tribune?* I did. And I'm mighty proud of it. The *Tribune* fairly licked its chops over it. And so did I, if you must know."

Beany stared dumfoundedly at him a full half-minute. Her lips were parted and the freckle cream, which she had used for ten nights running, went for naught, for the freckles stood out like flecks of butter in pale buttermilk. "You wrote it—for meanness. To get even with us. I—I never thought of *you*—writing it."

"Yes, I wrote it for meanness," he exulted. "To get even with you for making a sucker out of me. For having the whole school laughing up their sleeves at me. Or did you think you could step on a rattlesnake and have it smile back at you? And I'm not through. From now on, it's war to the hilt."

Beany turned stumblingly. For suddenly the smell in chem lab was nauseating. She muttered again. "I never thought of *you*—writing it," and hurried jerkily out of the room. She had to hold to the stair rail as she went down the familiar, yet unfamiliar, echoing stairs.

If she had looked back—which she didn't—she would have seen Norbett Rhodes standing, looking a little sickly, himself, at the cloudy mixture in the test tube. She would have heard his rickety pretense at a laugh. "I stand for justice. That malarkey!"

It didn't seem possible that in the brief time of Beany's stay inside Harkness the snow, which had fallen with such lethargic unconcern, could have changed to such a slanting white fury. It didn't seem to come from the sky but from some great snow supply piled up at the north.

Already Johnny's little car was iced over thickly. The engine sputtered with cold half-heartedness as Beany drove through the storm. Only part of Beany's mind was on her driving, as she coaxed the car through the drifts in the park. She felt flayed and sick. Now it was all over between her and Norbett.

She had to get out and wipe the snow off the windshield with her mittens before she turned onto College Boulevard. Only seven blocks on a stop-street before she turned onto Barberry and slunk up their driveway and into the garage. And she, Beany, would slink into the house.

She was crawling along the boulevard, with the one windshield wiper clickety-clicking, halting, then jerking into frenzied action. She was passing an intersection, when suddenly, without warning, a car's blurred headlights leaped out at her. They were right under her left window, right under her elbow—and, simultaneously, there was the crash of headlight glass in the oncoming car as the car gave her a thump broadside. A thump which sent Johnny's light car skidding clear over against the opposite curb.

As soon as the car settled, Beany tried to get out the door by the wheel. She pushed and pushed, but the bump had done something to the door. She couldn't open it. She climbed out the right side.

But there was no other car in sight. No person to emerge out of the pelting darkness. It was like a ghost car which had loomed up, smacked her, and disappeared in the snow and darkness.

She looked at her own car. No wonder the door on the driver's side wouldn't open. The door handle was off. Beany scuffed through the snow for it. She had to step back once to let a big coal truck go lumbering by. Again, as a florist's closed truck felt its way along. She found broken chunks of headlight glass, but no door handle.

She climbed shakily back behind the wheel. It wasn't my fault, she reassured herself. *I* was on a stop-street. This other car came busting out from a side street and hit *me*. . . . "Whenever you're involved in an accident, be sure and report it," was one of Martie Malone's slogans. "Right or wrong, report it."

But if she reported it, the police would find out that she was driving a car without a brake and light sticker. Johnny's car would be impounded. Now wouldn't that be something? For the daughter of Brake-and-light Malone, Impound-the-cars Malone, to have the car she was driving impounded? Wouldn't the *Tribune* headline that with glee? The ghostly driver in the ghostly car had gone blithely on his way. . . . So what was there to do but maneuver the car out from the curb and crawl on home?

She was still arguing with herself when she left Johnny's car in the dark haven of the garage. Part of her longed for the solace of telling. Maybe Elizabeth would say, "Beany, have you been driving Johnny's car?" . . . "Yes, and someone whammed into me."

But when she entered the kitchen on knees that were as strengthless as blanc mange, Elizabeth's head was buried in a big green towel. She flipped her wet hair back from her glowing face and said, as she rubbed her head hardily, "I've washed my hair, and will you put it up in pin curls? I'm going to try it a new way. I'll have to, if I get the hat I looked at up on the boulevard. Beany, remember the wide, sort of floppy hat I wore with my going-away suit? Don always liked it—and this one sits back on my head the same way. Only I wonder if it's too young for me. Martie, show Beany the new sailor suit I bought you."

"I am making frosting," little Martie returned, absorbed in beating water in a bowl.

Maybe Mary Fred would ask it. She would surely notice that she had come in from the garage and would ask, "Where you been, Beany?" . . . "Why, I went tearing like crazy up to Harkness in Johnny's car to ask a favor of Norbett Rhodes. And got laughed at for my pains. And got hit broadside on my way home."

But Mary Fred kept right on stirring something on the stove and tasting it. "It's split-pea soup, but it doesn't taste like yours, Beany. What is that indefinable flavor you impart to it?"

"I put a little sweet basil in it," Beany said flatly. "Have you seen the *Tribune?*"

"You mean that screaming story about Ander? Yes. But no one pays any attention to the *Tribune*. It has to make mountains out of molehills to fill up space."

Beany's saddle shoes were full of melted snow. Her hands that she pulled out of soggy mittens were wet and lavender-colored. She even climbed the stairs and stopped in John-ny's doorway. Johnny stilled his typewriter. Emerson

Worth was sitting beside him, reading over some typed pages. His eyes, under those bushy gray buttes of eyebrows, were bright and alert this evening.

Johnny said happily, "Guess what? The opening scene will be the little boy and a neighbor giving him a pair of rabbits as he starts West. We're going to use little Martie; he's just made to order for the part. And then the next scene, when the wagon arrives, they'll be pulling rabbits out of boots and water buckets—even out of his mother's bonnet."

"I always hated rabbits," Beany said vehemently.

"Whew!" Johnny went on, unheeding. "Got to drag Insomnia out of her stall, get her checked over, so as to start gathering up rabbits and sunbonnets—and the fellow at Civic Theatre said he'd lend me a sunrise."

Beany couldn't say, "I was in a traffic accident with your car," because Johnny, the conscientious, would say, "We'd better report it, Beany." Even if it meant having his car impounded, he'd say it.

She slunk back down the stairs. It hadn't hurt Johnny's car any. It was already so full of dents he wouldn't notice one more. And when the snow went off, she'd surely find the door handle. Just forget about it, Beany.

She had to do something. You forgot when you were busy. She stirred up some gingerbread. She put Elizabeth's damp and golden-brown hair up into myriad little snails, stuck through with bobby pins. After dinner, when she washed the dishes, she cleaned out the icebox. She found a carton and made Rosie O'Grady and her tumbling pups a warmer, softer bed.

If you did things you could forget.

But, just as Beany was sinking off to sleep that night,

she jerked to startled wide-awakeness. She was seeing again the blurred lights of a car right under her elbow, was hearing again the smash of glass, was feeling again the rocking impact that had slithered her little car over to the curb.

It takes another nail to pound out an embedded nail.

Fortunately, or unfortunately, another anxiety pushed out in Beany's mind the haunting, unfinished feeling of the car incident that snowy night. That is, *almost.* It was only at night that the memory of it sat waiting on her pillow.

It was Mary Fred's bewildered hurt, then her angry defiance, which crowded it out. Mary Fred had been wrong when she said, "Nobody pays any attention to the *Tribune*." She had been wrong when she said, "Oh, Lila's mother! You know what a crepe-hanger she is." Wrong, when she said, "The Delts are too big to pay attention to such a tempest in not even a teapot."

Every issue of the campus paper, *The Pioneer*, which Beany perused avidly, proved how wrong Mary Fred had been. Seething indignation was voiced, not only by the Pep Club but by the Student Council. There was much hue and cry about traditions threatened. The fraternities, the sororities, cast bitter recriminations at the mavericks on the campus. Ander Erhart, the ringleader of the rebellion, was a pariah.

Mary Fred was torn between loyalties. "Ander and I always eat together at the Clunch" (Campus lunchroom) "and I'm certainly not going to give him the brushoff now." She was torn between loyalties to Lila, to the Delts—to her own stubborn convictions. "It *is* a lot of fiddle-faddle. I don't blame the returned G.I.'s for rebelling," she said defiantly.

On Sunday Beany and Mary Fred attended mass together.

Kneeling beside her, Beany could see the tense supplication in Mary Fred's uplifted face. That "What shall I do? What shall I do?" indecision. They left the church and walked only part of the distance together.

Lila's mother had asked Mary Fred to stop and have Sunday breakfast with them. Both Beany and Mary Fred knew what was behind Mrs. Sears' insistent hospitality. They both knew that, along with the broiled grapefruit and muffins, Mary Fred would be served reproachful phrases, " . . . jeopardizing not only your own future but Lila's . . ." Lila, the leaner-on, the tagger-after.

"Beany, I don't want to hurt Lila," Mary Fred said wanly. "I don't know what to do. Well, say a prayer for me." And she walked up Lila's street.

I don't know either, Beany thought helplessly. If only I could do something. But what could a Harkness high-school sophomore do to stem or divert the tide of disapproval brought upon Mary Fred by her loyalty to Ander Erhart, the cowboy who had smashed tradition and jaws, as the *Tribune* put it. As that hateful Norbett Rhodes had put it. And then bragged about it. Beany was grateful to have something to hitch her anger to.

11

Hurry Home, Don!

The next day, Monday, Harkness High was turned into a noisy, milling stampede of thirteen hundred and twenty-seven pupils, banging lockers and shouting exuberantly. An unexpected holiday! The previous Saturday the Harkness football team had defeated their greatest rival and the principal had handed them a holiday as reward.

In the midst of the din and hullabaloo someone clutched Beany's arm desperately and Kay yelled in her ear, "Beany, can I go home with you? And see Rosie's pups?"

"Why sure, Kay."

Would Beany ever understand Kay? Beany had asked her before, and Kay had turned frozen-faced and said she was sorry but she couldn't.

But this was no Frozen-face who walked liltingly beside Beany down the school steps and through the park where the wind riffled the snow on the thinly frozen lake, and riffled Kay's long blond hair. Kay said, with a sober glance at the Park Gate Hotel, "I'll get home by three-thirty. Faye won't know we had a holiday. If I'd known we were going to have it, I'd have brought a brush I have. One of those stiff, bristly ones, but it's blue and Faye—well, it didn't match the colors in the bedroom. Rosie liked me to brush her. Are the pups still in your room, Beany?"

"Yes, we have to guard them from little Martie. He loves them too hard. When they get a little bigger we'll put them in the furnace room in the basement."

Thinking of little Martie brought up the thought of Elizabeth—Elizabeth, of the anxious eyes. Elizabeth, ever waiting. "Kay, about Elizabeth—I mean, she's twenty-two, but she doesn't look as young as your mother. She's been so worried. When she graduated from Harkness they said in the Year Book about her:

> *She is debonair and pretty,*
> *She is full of pep and witty,*
> *And how we love her!*

I wish she'd take dancing and make skating costumes for herself. I wish she'd have good times like Faye."

Kay only gave her an odd look, which Beany didn't even see because it was just at that moment that a daring thought popped into her mind. Why couldn't she, Beany, telephone to Don out in San Francisco and tell him he just had to get on home? Don had written to Elizabeth that he would be detained at Letterman Hospital for treatment for awhile. "You know army red tape," he had said, "so just hold everything." But she, Beany, would tell him he *had* to cut through the red tape and get transferred or whatever he had to do. Why, that was it. Just the first chance she got when Elizabeth was out of the house, she would take matters into her own hands.

Red came running out of the driveway with his tail-wag-
ging welcome. "Here's the homestead," Beany said.

"Oh, Beany, your house is the most beautiful I've ever
seen," Kay said. No, Beany couldn't understand Kay. Their
house beautiful? Their house—sitting between the starched
and preening residence of Mrs. Socially-prominent Adams and the brushed, polished, judicial one of Judge Buell?

"You've always lived here, haven't you, Beany?" Kay
asked.

"From cradle to Harkness," Beany agreed. "My room
looks pretty junior high, compared to yours and Faye's.
But I'm going to do it over."

"But you did it yourself," Kay marveled. "I've lived so
many places. But I've never had a room of my own where
I could do what I wanted to."

That whole day surprised Beany. This was a different
Kay from the one who walked through Harkness halls with
her pinned-on smile; different, even, from the acquiescent
Kay who sat in the Park Gate apartment while her mother
bubbled on gaily. This Kay let out a glad, gurgling cry at
sight of Rosie and her waddling four and sank down on the
floor with no thought of her lemon-yellow sweater or im-
maculate gray skirt as they climbed and romped over her.
This Kay's face shone when little Martie sidled up to her
and said, "I like you."

"I like you, too," she assured him.

Today was not what the family called one of Emerson
Worth's "lost-spike days." Today he was just an older,
frailer edition of the Emerson Worth whose editorials had
helped to shape the West. Johnny said it was his three
square meals a day at the Malone table which made his

vague days less frequent. "The silver spike was drowned in your split-pea soup, Beany," Johnny said.

Emerson Worth acknowledged Beany's introduction to Kay with his old bluntness. "Kay? What's that a nickname of?"

"Katherine."

"Then I'll call you Katherine. Kay is no name."

"Don't mind him," Beany whispered apologetically.

And Kay didn't mind. "I like to be called Katherine. My father always called me that. Only Faye thought that it would be—well, cute for us to be Faye and Kay."

"My name is Catherine with a *C*," Beany said. "But when I was a baby, Johnny was two and he couldn't say 'Baby' so he called me something that sounded like Beany."

Kay and Elizabeth—even as Kay and little Martie—fell in love at first sight. Beany was almost jealous of the adoration in Kay's eyes for Elizabeth.

Elizabeth followed up Kay's remark about her father with a gentle question. "Is your father living, Katherine?"

"Yes. Yes—he's a mining engineer in a little town in Utah." She was silent a moment and then she turned impulsively to Elizabeth. "Supposing your husband, Don—supposing he had to work in some awful little town where the wind blows black dirt that made your hair dingy—and you had to do your own laundry—and they never had any good shows—and the people were all old busybodies, would you stay there with him?"

Elizabeth laughed chokily, "Would I? I'd follow him to the Cape of Good Hope. I'd wash clothes on rocks in the river—I'd hobnob with the head hunters if I could be with Don."

Elizabeth went back to her mixing of chocolate brownies

in the kitchen. The lighted oven, as usual, was smokily reminiscent of the last thing baked in it; this time of the scalloped potatoes that had bubbled over in baking for Sunday's dinner. Elizabeth asked, "Beany, what happened to those shelled pecans that were here in the cupboard— you know, in the cellophane bag?"

"I'll bet Johnny ate them," Beany passed judgement, after a fruitless pushing about of spices, vanilla, and boxes of breakfast food.

Beany's judgement proved correct. For when Johnny was called in from the garage, he temporized, "Well—I ate a few."

Elizabeth giggled. "Here, hollow-legs, you can finish up these brownies I put away the last time I made them."

Elizabeth always saved back some of the lumpy chocolate-covered squares from each baking, hoping that Don would be home. Brownies were Don's favorite sweet. Ever since she had received Don's wire, Elizabeth had been baking brownies hopefully. . . . Beany was shaken again by that same impatient fury. Why didn't Don hurry and come home? Didn't Don know about the new suit Elizabeth had ready to meet him in? Didn't Don know that Elizabeth was debating on that picture hat up on the boulevard? Beany could visualize Elizabeth in the new suit and the picture hat, going with Don to all the gay festivities of Homecoming. Just as soon as I can get Elizabeth out of the house, I'm going to telephone Don and tell him how hard this waiting is on Elizabeth. . . .

Johnny was saying, "This holiday is an unexpected blessing. I'm taking Insomnia up to Mac's for my brake and light sticker. Only, there's an unsolved mystery. What happened to the door handle on the driver's side? I knew it was loose, but I didn't expect it to drop off. Or walk off. I've looked all over the garage for it. You don't suppose someone thought it was a museum piece?"

Beany felt that old familiar roiliness inside. The door handle that had been knocked off when a strange car had thumped into her! Even after the snow had melted she hadn't been able to find it there at the intersection.

Johnny was saying, "I can get you some more pecans. I'm going up to Mac's right away—and I'll go past the store."

Elizabeth laughed. "Should we trust him, Beany?"

Beany shook off her uneasy thoughts. "No," she said firmly. No—Johnny would come home with all they had in the store. "You go, Elizabeth—" Why, maybe this was her chance to look after Elizabeth by telephoning Don at San Francisco! "It's nice out, Elizabeth, and you could take Martie—" Martie's short legs would keep it from being a hurried dash to the store and back. "Oh, and Kay, why don't you go with her? Elizabeth wants someone else to pass on the hat. She's afraid it's too schoolgirlish for her."

It resulted as Beany hoped it would—with Elizabeth and Kay and the snow-suited Martie setting out.

Now, Beany said to herself resolutely, as the front door closed behind them. Somehow, it was a little frightening to telephone San Francisco.

She stretched the telephone cord from its stand into the privacy of the closet under the stairs. She didn't want Emerson Worth or Johnny to come bolting in and overhear. She put in a call for Lieutenant Donald McCallin at Letterman Hospital in San Francisco. She had a worrying time of waiting, fearful that Elizabeth would come from the store before the call came from San Francisco.

But the call came first. Huddled there in the stuffy wrap closet, Beany finally heard a man's faraway voice ask, "Is this you, Elizabeth?"

"It's Beany, Don. Elizabeth isn't here right now. Look, Don," she said loudly, urgently, "I called you because Elizabeth is—is grieving so about your not coming home. Can't you come on right away?"

"Well, Beany—I thought maybe—"

"But you can, can't you? I can hardly hear you, Don." It wasn't that his voice sounded faraway as much as it sounded tired and wabbly.

"I suppose I could—only I thought—"

"Oh, please do, Don! Elizabeth says she's getting pointed ears like a bird dog, just waiting to hear from you. She's even getting thin. She's waited so long—"

There was a thoughtful silence and then the same thin, uncertain voice said, "All I was thinking about was—was Elizabeth's happiness. Because I could stay here—"

Beany didn't wait for him to finish. "Then come home as quick as ever you can. Get transferred or whatever you have to do. Nothing matters to Elizabeth except your coming home."

"Maybe you're right, Beany—maybe nothing else would matter."

"You send a wire—because she's got a new suit to wear— Oh gee, here she comes now! Be sure, Don."

Beany was thankful for Martie's stumbling inadequacy on the steps to delay their entrance. The telephone was back on its stand. Elizabeth carried a hatbox. It won't be long now before you'll be wearing it, Beany exulted. Somebody has to look after the Malones. . . . Now if only I could *do* something about Mary Fred.

.

The whole day Kay rode through on a wave of excited, stolen rapture. "Does the school often have holidays like this?" she asked, as they ate toasted cheese and bacon sandwiches at noon.

"Once," Johnny remembered, "the heating system went haywire and we had two free days."

"If only the heating system would go haywire again!" Kay said fervently.

At three-fifteen Kay took her farewell of Rosie and her four. A lingering patting of the brown dog that she had named Pierre. "He can be your dog and we'll take care of him for you," Beany promised.

Beany walked as far as the park with her. Kay was sober now—troubled. "Beany, don't mention my spending the day at your house to—to—well, to anybody." Beany wanted to ask why, but Kay's eyes were too clouded.

"I won't," she agreed.

At the park entrance, Beany said, "Good-bye, Katherine—come again."

Kay said, "Good-bye, Catherine! I will—oh, I will—" and suddenly she threw her arms around Beany, pressed her face close to hers—and ran on across the park to the Park Gate Hotel.

Beany put her hand wonderingly to her cheek where Kay, whom Harkness called Frozen-face, had left a wet tear-smudge.

While Beany walked partway with Kay, Elizabeth had callers.

Beany saw the nice gray car parked in their driveway at the house's front door. Johnny, driving in with his dented and scabrous little car, couldn't get past it. He called to

Beany as she started up the steps, "Go in there and tell whoever that is to get their tin can out of my way."

But Beany didn't because she could sense, the minute
she stepped into the front hall, something a little hushed,
something very significant about the presence of the three
girls in the living room with Elizabeth.

She felt it, too, when Elizabeth came out into the kitchen
and said, "Beany, would you make some tea?" Even
Elizabeth's voice wasn't casual. "Use the silver teapot and
the matching sugar and creamer. And put some brownies on
a plate."

"Who are they?" Beany asked low.

"Three girls from the Delts."

"Oh!" Beany said. So they had come to talk to Elizabeth,
a Delt alum, about Mary Fred! "You mean they've come to
talk about Ander—and Mary Fred eating lunch with him?"

Elizabeth's smile was twisted. "No names are being
mentioned. It's all on a very high plane."

Hurriedly, nervously, Beany dumped a half-cup of sugar
into the small, silver sugar bowl that went with the tea set;
she sliced a lemon; she picked out the most perfect brownies
and put them on the silver cake plate. She even put on some
of the lump sugar they had been saving. As though the best
was none too good for the girls who held Mary Fred's fate
in their hands.

And then, balancing it all on the tray, Beany carried it
in. She tried to be as graciously nonchalant in acknowledg-
ing the introductions as Elizabeth was in making them. But
their names were a blur. She was in a hurry to get out. What
were they saying—oh, what were they saying in their nice,
modulated voices? Were those tinkly laughs really laughs or
just a polite way of leavening conversation?

Beany stood in the back hall and heard their leavetaking. Straining her ears, she heard one say, "We're glad we've had this little talk with you, Elizabeth. I'm sure you understand our position," and Elizabeth's noncommittal, "Thank you so much for coming."

Hurrying back into the kitchen, Beany almost bumped into Mary Fred who stood stiffly erect, watching the gray car drive up to the wide cement apron in front of the garage, turn around, and whirr gently out. She and Lila had come in the back way. Watching, Mary Fred's lips drew in a tight, ugly line.

Beany said placatingly, "They came to call on Elizabeth."

"They *would,*" Mary Fred said shortly.

Elizabeth came out of the living room, carrying the sugar bowl. She was laughing as she said, "Beany, we'll have to remember and look in the sugar bowl after this. It seems to be little Martie's favorite hiding place. Look what one of the girls dipped out." In the sugar shell Elizabeth held up was an agate which Johnny had given the little boy.

Mary Fred said grimly, "Girls have been turned down by a sorority for less than a marble in the sugar bowl. . . . I suppose they came, all flowery, high-flown phrases, which, sifted down, means that unless Mary Fred Malone toes the chalk mark they will have none of Mary Fred."

Elizabeth said, "Come on in, all of you, and we'll finish the tea party."

Through the big bay windows, the rosy westering sun pushed fullhearted into the Malone living room, making the red leather redder and showing clearly the worn spots in the rugs. Elizabeth poured tea for them all—Lila, Mary Fred, Beany, even little Martie. Beany had to dash back to

the kitchen to get more cups and spoons, and an unbreak-
able plastic cup for the little boy. And she was glad—glad
not to have to look at Mary Fred's stony face.

Mary Fred sat on the curved window seat under the
arched, six-windowed bay, half-turned so that only her set
profile showed against the pink and lavender and crimson
sky.

"Let me get you some hot tea, Mary Fred," Beany insisted. "And the brownies are so good—lots of pecans in
them." . . . She meant, Let me do something for you so
you won't ache so inside. I know how you feel. Just as
though something were broken, and every time you move
it hurts. That's the way it was with me after the Biddinger
kids left—and then when Jock and Lorna tore off without
even waving good-by . . .

"No thanks, Beany." . . . She meant, No thanks, Beany,
tea and brownies can't fill the emptiness inside me. . .

Silence fell on the little group.

Lila, with her fur coat half sliding off her shoulders,
looked in drawn sympathy at Mary Fred. The Sears family
were what Mrs. No-complaint termed "well-fixed," and
Lila was an only child. Lila's mother had had her mink coat
cut down for Lila and relined beautifully with gold bro-
caded satin, on the premise that Lila would be a sorority
girl. But the coat looked heavy on Lila's thin shoulders.
The rich brown fur tended to make Lila's nondescript
brown hair look more spiritless.

And finally Mary Fred stood up. "Go ahead, Elizabeth,
shoot the works!" she challenged with an ugly laugh. "I've
heard it from the Delts, from my upperclass counselor,
from Lila's mother. Tell me how dreary college life is for
a girl who doesn't make a sorority. Tell me how fortunate

I was that the Delts looked my way. Tell me nothing else matters for a girl in college—why, what chance has a girl on the campus to be *anybody* if she hasn't got a sorority pin? Tell me how it was the happiest event in *your* life. Go on, tell me how I'll disgrace the family if I don't heel when the Delts say heel. What is a little thing like disloyalty to a friend—or—or compromising your own principles in order to make a sorority—" her voice thinned, broke.

Elizabeth reached forward to stay little Martie's hand. "No, Martie—no, you can't have any more cookies." She put the plate on the mantel out of his reach. . . . She said, as though she were thinking aloud, "The sorority meant a lot to me. 'It is meet and salutary,' as it says in the prayer book, to be in the swim at school, to soak up all the good times you can. Remember, Beany and Mary Fred, when I gave a Delt candlelight tea here in this big room?"

She paused and went thoughtfully on, "And then, before I knew it, I was married. Don went to war. Little Martie was born. I lay awake night after night. And was it easier because I was a sorority girl? No, it wasn't. What I'm trying to say, Mary Fred sweet, is that I'm not telling you what to do. I can't. You'll have to decide that. It's true that for some girls running with the herd is the happiest way. It'd be tough for them to go it alone. That's all, Mary Fred."

"I know," Mary Fred said raggedly, without even looking Lila's way. Now all Mary Fred's angry defiance was gone. There was only indecision and great hurt. "I liked the Delts. I thought they liked me and wanted me because I was myself. But they don't—they want the Mary Fred Malone that looks like me—but they don't want what I'm like inside and that—that's what hurts—"

Suddenly Lila flung off the weighty mink coat and stood up. "Mary Fred, you poor sap, if you're thinking of me— and that long line mother gave you—don't! Don't, Mary Fred! You're *you*—and that's all that counts. It counts more than my making a sorority—it does, Mary Fred. Stop thinking about *me*—" Lila, the leaner-on, was saying magnanimously, "Go your own way, Mary Fred, and let me fumble along the best I can."

Beany rattled the cups over Mary Fred's mumbled and thick, "Thanks, Lila—thanks a lot."

Beany tried to sort out her thoughts as she stacked the saucers, as she grabbed up the napkins. Part of her was a fierce, fighting fury at the Delts. But the other part was cringing over Mary Fred's being hurt. She would go on being loyal to Ander because she couldn't compromise. And she would go on being hurt.

But there was another way. It was so simple. Why hadn't Beany thought of it before? Of course, Mary Fred wouldn't avoid Ander. But supposing Ander diligently avoided Mary Fred? It wouldn't be for long. Just till Homecoming at the end of the month. Surely Ander could do that.

Again Beany's square jaw set resolutely. I'll explain it all to Ander; a man doesn't realize these things. . . . Oh, Mary Fred, we'll keep you from sticking your neck out. We'll get you in the Delts yet! . . .

12

Return of the Hero

Often Johnny, twirling the radio dials to get a newscast, would catch the tail-end of one of the radio serials. "There's an exciting surprise in store for you, gang, so don't miss—" the fervor-pitched voice of the announcer would exhort before the dial spun.

Sometimes it seemed to Beany that that phrase could be applied to life in the Malone household: "There's an exciting surprise in store for you."

Beany was so sound asleep that early dawn in middle November that when Red whimpered in the hall outside her door the sound merely merged into the fabric of her dreams. But when he pushed her door open—evidently the only bedroom door he found that would push open—and put his paws up on her bed and nosed imperatively at her face she had to rouse. Rosie gave a few short, perturbed barks, but Red, in dog language, conveyed to her that this was no barking affair.

At the sound of a car in their side driveway, Beany stumbled to her window. A yellow taxi was backing up, turning around in the open space in front of their garage. It roared swiftly out of the driveway. As Beany bent to pick up the fallen sweater that she had washed the night before and left to dry on the table beside the radiator, she heard someone trying the locked front door. Oh, now where was that quilted calico robe of hers?

By the time she found it and started down the stairs, squirming into it—one sleeve would be wrongside out!— she heard someone coming in the side door which opened into the back hall. The basement door, they called it, because it opened onto a landing from which stairs went to the basement and from which three steps led to the hall.

Beany stopped in startled fright in the hallway. A soldier on crutches was making a halting entrance. She could barely see—or perhaps hear the clink of—some metal contraption extending beyond the cast his foot was in.

"I'm Don, Mary Fred—"

"I'm not Mary Fred. I'm Beany."

"Oh, you're Beany! I forgot how grownup you'd be by now."

Beany stood there stupidly, her sleep-fogged mind trying to adjust. Don? Elizabeth's Don? This thin, sick-looking man, hanging shakily onto his crutches? This wasn't the erect, broad-shouldered Lieutenant McCallin who had walked down the chapel aisle under crossed swords with Elizabeth. This wasn't the pictured Lieutenant McCallin whose eyes twinkled out of the picture on Elizabeth's dresser. This was a thin, drained-faced, crippled soldier who was saying, "Had to leave my duffle bag outside. I'm sorry the transport got in at such an ungodly hour."

"I thought you'd send a wire."

"I didn't know what time I'd land, Beany, or I would have. I got a chance for the plane ride and I grabbed it."

Beany was mumbling, "But—Elizabeth was going to meet you—in her new suit—and the big hat she said she bet you'd like, because it was big and floppy like her going-away hat. And we were going to have fried chicken and ice cream." All this for the return of the hero.

Don didn't take those three steps up into the hall where Beany stood. His teeth were chattering weakly. He swayed unsteadily and said, "Beany, I guess you'll have to give me a hand. And oh lord, kid, could I have a cup—of—hot coffee?"

"Don, you're sick!"

"I'm not too good. . . . Beany, are you sure you're right—about Elizabeth," he entreated, suddenly unnerved, "about her wanting me to come home even if—"

Beany didn't have to answer that. A door opened upstairs and footsteps came running down the stairs. Elizabeth, in her red wool housecoat, the black velvet buttons buttoned in crooked haste, her lovely straggled hair framing the breathtaking hope in her face. "Don—oh, Don—you're back! You've come home—"

Beany walked out of the hall, her eyes blinking with tears. It didn't seem right to watch, even in the bronze half-light of dawn, the hurting ecstasy of that meeting. For her to hear the choked, "Elizabeth—beloved, beloved—"

The next day at Harkness, during the noisy bedlam of lunch period, it was Kay Maffley who caught a glimpse of Beany's blurred eyes in the mirror on the inside of her locker door. It was Kay who reached out to her and said,

"Beany, Beany, you've been crying! What's the matter?"

"It's Don," Beany said, sobbing outright. "He came home—before daylight this morning. Elizabeth had to help him up—those three steps into the hall. And he couldn't walk upstairs—Elizabeth had to fix him a bed on the davenport. And he isn't really—home. He has to report to the hospital here—today. Maybe—oh, Kay, maybe they're going to have to amputate his leg at the knee—"

Kay wasn't the talky kind. But her arm was tight around Beany as Beany, her sack of lunch clutched to her, started automatically toward the clattering din of the lunchroom. As they came to Miss Hewlitt's empty classroom, Kay said gently, "Let's duck in here. Miss Hewlitt wouldn't care if you ate your lunch here."

"I don't want any lunch," Beany choked. She sat on top of the first desk and burst out, as she blew her nose, "I thought I was helping Elizabeth when I called up Don and just *made* him come home. He told Elizabeth he had intended staying out in Frisco at Letterman and having his leg operation there. He said he hated to think of her going through all the worry. Then he said he weakened when I called him up—and he got transferred to the soldiers' hospital here."

Kay said, "I'm glad you called him. It's better—it's better for Elizabeth. I think she's guessed all along that Don was keeping something from her."

But Beany wasn't listening. She blew her nose again—angrily, resentfully. "Why is it, Kay, that every time I try to save any of the family it just backfires? Like Johnny. I tried to steer him away from Emerson's book. I showed him that it was likely to be a hopeless race with time. I was so afraid that if something happened to Emerson, Johnny would be brokenhearted. And what good did it do? It just gave him the idea of putting Emerson's book material into this play. So now Johnny's running his legs off getting all those freighters' boots, and a lot of rabbits, and a bustle for the teacher—sounds like a song, doesn't it?" she said with a choked laugh, " 'A bustle for the teacher—' "

Kay laughed softly. "You'd better mark off Johnny as hopeless."

"I have," Beany agreed grimly. "Johnny and Emerson both. Though if it hadn't been for Emerson, we'd still have Mrs. No-complaint, and I wouldn't have peanut butter sandwiches in my lunch every day. . . . And then I tried to help Mary Fred by taking Norbett to Miss Hewlitt's, and he heard about it. That's why he wrote that hateful write-up about Ander. That's why he acts as though I—I had a harelip or something. Not that I care," Beany hastened to add, "not that I care a hoot if he doesn't ever speak to me."

Day after day Beany Malone and Norbett Rhodes sat beside each other in typing class like strangers—worse than strangers, for there was the constant memory of Norbett's parting words, "You've made a sucker out of me for the last time. From now on it's war to the hilt."

Beany mused, "If it hadn't been for that mess, Mary Fred would be all set for the Delts' pledging. And then I thought I could make everything hunky-dory by talking to Ander—and Ander was so nice. Honest, Ander was so sweet," she repeated.

"I know," Kay said.

Beany had told Kay about that. How the very next day after she had resolved to appeal to Ander she had bumped into him, buying notebook paper at Downey's drugstore, and had told him she wanted to talk to him. How Ander had bought her a chocolate nut sundae, and had even filled in her faltering gaps. "Ander, it's about Mary Fred and her—her—"

"—her keeping in the good graces of the Delts?" he had said.

"That's it," Beany said relievedly. "And on account of you being sort of—sort of—"

"—tarred and feathered as a renegade," he had helped her out again.

"Yes, and if Mary Fred goes with you—I mean eats lunch with you, and walks across the campus with you, she'll be—well—"

"—tarred with the same black brush, you mean. I know it, and I'm not happy about it. I've even told Mary Fred—but, well you know Mary Fred."

Beany had leaned earnestly across the blue marbleized linoleum table top. "Of course I know Mary Fred. But why couldn't *you* avoid *her?* Just on the campus? Just till Homecoming is over? Because, Ander, I can't bear to think of her being left out of all those Friday teas and Sunday morning breakfasts at the Delt house. And not being freshman escort to the Homecoming queen. Lila told me she was slated to be—"

Ander's blue eyes had flashed. "You mean she'd be done out of that, too?"

"Oh yes! No one has ever been an escort—or a queen—without a sorority backing her. For years the freshmen escorts have all been Delts. The Delts put in Elizabeth, you know. And Mary Fred could wear her dress." Beany glupped her spoon into the chocolate and nut mixture and thought fleetingly of that pale blue diaphanous dress with the spattering of velvet roses appliqued on the skirt. "Every

year the escorts wear the same—or else the same type of
dress. They stick to tradition on the campus."

"So I've discovered," Ander had said with a grim quirk.
"Okay, Beany, I'll run from Mary Fred like a rope-shy
bronc. I know when she has her lunch and what time she
goes to classes. My shadow will never darken her path."

Kay reached out and touched Beany's hand. She said
comfortingly, "I think you were wonderful to save Mary
Fred through Ander."

"But it didn't do any good," Beany said bitterly. "I
could have saved my breath—and Ander could have saved
himself my chocolate nut sundae."

"It didn't? Didn't Ander run from her like a rope-shy
bronc?"

Beany laughed shortly. "Not fast enough for Mary Fred."

Kay reached into Beany's sack of lunch and unwrapped
the double triangle of peanut butter sandwich. "Here,
Beany, you'd better eat something. Eat half your sandwich
and I'll eat half. . . . What did Mary Fred do?"

Beany took an unrelishing bite out of the sandwich.

"Mrs. No-complaint Adams used to make the best minced
ham for sandwiches," she remembered wistfully. . . .
"Why, Mary Fred, as Lila says, threw down the gauntlet."

"Honest!" Kay breathed.

"She didn't need to," Beany grieved. "Lila told me
about it yesterday. It was the day before yesterday, and
Lila and Mary Fred and four of the Delts started over to
the Clunch. And then the Dean of Women stopped Mary
Fred to ask her about—I forget what Lila said she wanted to
ask her about," Beany said in an "it doesn't matter anyway"
voice. "Lila said she and the Delts went on and they found
a table at the Clunch and saved a place for Mary Fred. But

she was a long time coming. Lila said, in the meantime,
Ander had come in and taken his tray clear over to a table
in the corner—"

"I feel so sorry for Ander," Kay put in.

"—and then Mary Fred came in. Lila said she looked
over the lunchroom—it was just packed, Lila said—and
saw Ander sitting at a table by himself. Lila and the girls
were almost through their dessert, but they all yelled to
Mary Fred to join them but—"

"Oh, m'gosh," Kay said, "I know what she did."

"I knew, too," Beany groaned. "I knew even before Lila
told me. I could just see Mary Fred picking up her tray and
walking past the Delts and Lila, with her chin stuck out.
I could just see her putting her tray down beside Ander."

"Oh, Beany," Kay said, "I think she was wonderful."

Oddly enough that was just what Lila had said. Lila,
standing with her thin ends of hair clinging to the rich
sheen of her fur coat, with her timid eyes lighted in memory
of Mary Fred's courage; "Oh, Beany," she had breathed,
"I think she was wonderful!" . . .

"But you see, Kay," Beany summed it all up despairingly,
"I try to make things easier for them—and it doesn't work
out. It's just as though there was a pattern—and I can't
change it."

Kay said slowly, "Maybe there is a pattern, Beany—a
Malone pattern. Some folks—like you Malones—aren't the
kind to lock their doors, or their hearts, or—or," she added,
"or to run away from hard things."

The halls were taking on the active hubbub that meant
that pupils were returning from lunch period. Beany's
fifth-hour typing was next. An aftermath of sob—like a
jerking hiccough—shook her coral-colored sweater. She

said in the thin, gravelly voice that is left after a hard cry has spent itself, "Golly, Kay, I feel just like Stella Dallas on the radio, sobbing out my life story. I hate to think of next hour—but I have to get some memory sentences turned in. I hate to go in there, looking all bleary-eyed." . . . I hate to have Norbett see me, looking like a drooping sob sister, she thought. . . .

"Here," Kay said, reaching for her own cloisonne compact. Beany submitted, like a child, while Kay flipped the wafer-sized and very clean powder puff over her face, while Kay gently etched Beany's swollen lips with lipstick. "Now smile, Beany."

But that Beany could not do. She burst out desolately, "Always when I do these things for the family, I ask myself, 'What would Faye do?' You know she said the only way to keep happy and carefree was to keep from getting into a spot that would make trouble. I keep wanting Mary Fred and Elizabeth to be like her."

Kay opened her lips to say something, and then looked away. As though either fright or loyalty—or both—kept her lips sealed.

Beany sat in Miss Meigs' typing class, her feet on the floor, her back straight, her elbows at an even keel with the typewriter. She kept her eyes, still smarting as though sand were in them, fastened on the propped-up page, and typed with weak fingers:

If you want a certain thing, the law is that you must work for it.

You will not fail if you never allow circumstances to limit endeavor.

So many of these memory sentences made life sound so black and white. So many of these proddings disclaimed entirely the complexities that went on in the heart. Complexities made by a tall boy, with hair the color of an Irish setter, with a clear-cut, mordant profile, sitting next to you and whacking away on his Woodstock.

Beany made a mistake. She sat there, listlessly debating whether to erase the spelled-wrong "endeavor" or whether to start a new page. (No more than three erasures on a page, Miss Meigs always reminded them.) She was careful to keep her face averted so that Norbett wouldn't have the satisfaction of seeing her red-rimmed, bleary eyes. She even blew her nose warily.

Suddenly Norbett thrust a folded newspaper before her and demanded, "Did you see that in the morning paper? Looks like someone took up the cudgels in defense of your cowboy maverick."

Beany's eyes focused on the newspaper column which she had missed reading in the hurry-skurry of the morning.

It was on the page devoted to "Letters from Our Readers." This letter was titled, "Are Traditions Necessarily Holy?" and it wanted to know why serious-minded adult students should take part in the campus horseplay that was labeled tradition. It scoffed at the Varsity paper being *The Pioneer*, when it might better be called *The Parrot*. It reminded every reader that the G.I.'s, who had fought for democracy, were entitled to start new traditions— bigger and better ones. The letter was signed, "A Lover of Justice."

If Beany hadn't been so bent on not letting Norbett see that she had been crying, she might have seen that Norbett's eyes were both hopeful and quizzical. But Beany heard only his mocking voice, saying, "Can't you give three cheers for the Lover of Justice who took his pen in hand?"

Beany couldn't even answer. For she suddenly realized that the sobs she had thought securely packed away for the day could come tumbling out if she opened her lips. And what could be worse than for Norbett to see her cry? For Norbett to sit and gloat over a weeping Malone?

And so, she didn't open her lips at all. But turning her head far to the southeast she furiously attacked her memory sentence.

If you want a certain thing, the law is—

A week passed—a week from the day Beany had sobbed out her hopeless grief to Kay; a week from the day Norbett had thrust under her red eyes the letter from a Lover of Justice. That latter had reopened the controversy on the campus and started the wind blowing, at first gently and then more strongly, in the other direction. Other letters followed it. Thoughtful letters, irate letters. Letters that challenged the student body, letters that shamed them.

A week passed, and Beany, returning from school, found Mary Fred tussling with the folding ironing board in the butler's pantry (in which a butler had never trod.) "Now which of these leg-things do you pull out first?" Mary Fred asked.

And then Beany noticed that Mary Fred had thrown over a chair's back the pale blue, filmy dress Elizabeth had worn four years ago when she was freshman escort to the queen. The dress of timeless fashion with its fitted bodice and skirt, bouffant as an upside-down hollyhock. The queen, sitting in her gold throne chair, always wore white with a long train, while the escorts, like bridesmaids, wore flower shades of blue, peach, yellow, and green.

"Do you suppose if I dampened these velvet roses they would water-spot?" Mary Fred asked. Her voice was neither sober nor elated.

Beany asked in a not-daring-to-hope breathlessness, "What are you pressing it for, Mary Fred?"

Mary Fred chanted:

If you're waking, call me early,
Call me early, mother dear.
For I'm to be escort to the queen of Homecoming—

Have you forgotten, Beany, my pet, that today was the day they voted on the escorts?"

"Mary Fred, stop prancing. Do you really mean it? You were chosen?"

Mary Fred's prancing flippancy dropped. She said heavily, "Yes, I was chosen—not unanimously, you understand—but by a scant majority, to be freshman escort to the Homecoming queen."

"Oh, then your Delts—?"

"Not *my* Delts, honey. I was voted in in spite of the Delts. Not because of them. I got enough votes from the student body. Whether it was owing to the letters in the *Call*, which made some of them decide not to be sheep, or whether it was my own inimitable charm is anybody's guess. Yes," she repeated bleakly, "the campus okayed me, but not the Delts. So Mary Fred Malone will ride on the float behind the Varsity band, standing to the left of the queen's throne. Mary Fred will be wearing a corsage of gardenias, but they will not have been sent by the dear old sorority according to dear old hallowed custom."

"But you're freshman escort! Aren't you happy, Mary Fred?"

"Ask me something easy, Beany," Mary Fred said with a quivery smile. She picked up the blue cloud of dress and stood riffling the skirt absently above her scuffed, low-heeled brogues. "The voting was such a narrow squeak. All the Delt votes went for a nice docile lamb from the Delt fold." Again that bleak, hurt look came into her eyes. "And the queen—I heard, via the grapevine, that she is very, very disgruntled at having a lowly Independent for one of her attendants. But anyway," she added, with thin satisfaction, "I haven't—and I quote, 'jeopardized Lila's whole future.' "

"How do you know, Mary Fred?"

"Lila received her crested, engraved bid from the Delts yesterday. Mamma Sears has hurried her down to get a flu shot today so Lila can't possibly be sick and miss any of the festivities."

"But Mary Fred," Beany said eagerly, "I'll just bet anything that the Delts will change their mind about you. After your being chosen freshman escort. I'll bet later on they'll take you in. We'll all go down from Harkness and cheer like crazy for you when you go by on the float. Here, Mary Fred, I'll press your dress for you. And then you try it on. And you can wear that new pair of nylons I got for my birthday."

Mary Fred didn't answer. Even when Beany took the dress out of her arms, Mary Fred stood, staring ahead, braced as though a strong wind were blowing against her.

13

Growing Up Is Churning Up

The Friday of the big Homecoming parade in late November!

The sun shone down, warm and kind as a benison, even though snow still clung to streets in the residence districts. High schools would dismiss classes early so that students could line the downtown streets and cheer the football float, the sorority and fraternity floats, the alumni float and, above all, the float bearing the queen and her escorts. For this float floral companies had sent great masses of chrysanthemums—deep yellow ones, white ones. White and gold were the Varsity colors.

The parade, of course, was merely the opening gun for the two days of open-house hospitality on the campus; for the open doors over which waved "Welcome Old Grads" banners.

But neither Elizabeth nor Donald McCallin would stand in any of those receiving lines to shake hands with

alumni and faculty, and later to balance teacups on plates.
For the day of the Homecoming parade was the day the
surgeons at the Veterans' Hospital had decided to operate
on Lieutenant McCallin's leg, torn by a piece of flak.

On that day Beany hurried to overtake Kay Maffley on
Harkness' stairs. "Kay, I'm leaving school early. I told
you about Don. And I don't want Elizabeth sitting alone
out there at the hospital. You know how dreary it is waiting
while someone is in the operating room. So will you hand in
my theme on the UNO conference to Miss Hewlitt?"

"Beany, wait! Let me go with you. Oh, please—I want
to go with you. I can't bear to think of Elizabeth out there—
waiting alone. How are you going?"

"Carlton Buell said I could take his car. Johnny is using
his—I think he's going to gather up all those rabbits he'll
be needing in the second scene of the first act. Did I ever
tell you how I hated rabbits? Even old Frank, my rabbit
at home. Someone gave him to me one Easter when he was
just a tiny little thing—and he just grew and grew. Al-
though, I will say he's smarter than most rabbits."

And so Kay, too, was excused from Lit by an understanding Miss Hewlitt. Kay walked beside Beany as she hunted
through the parked cars for Carlton's roadster. In front
of Carlton's car was parked Johnny's little jalopy, the only
new thing about it being the brake and light sticker, which
had been issued that Monday of Harkness' football holiday.

Norbett Rhodes was bending over the hood of Johnny's
car, looking intently at the date on the brake and light
sticker. That old familiar, never-easing queasiness came
over Beany. Even with the bland sun on her head and
shoulders, she pulled her reversible close, as though she
were feeling the snowy fury of that night when the wind-

shield of Johnny's car had no brake and light sticker stuck firmly on it.

And, because of that queasiness, she spoke with acid politeness to Norbett, "Could we help you, Norbett—in case the date isn't quite clear enough for you to read?"

Norbett, the boy of surprises! He answered almost roughly, "Why didn't Johnny get that sticker sooner?"

"He got it as soon as he could," she answered, with that same mocking overemphasis on politeness. "There's that little rule, in case you don't remember, about a garage man checking a car first. Or did you still think you bought them by the package?"

What skullduggery did Norbett have up his sleeve that he should be sleuthing about looking at Johnny's car? Could he know about the accident that night? Oh why, Beany regretted for perhaps the four hundred and nine-teenth time, didn't I tell the family about it? Why didn't I report it? Then I wouldn't have this unfinished, sword-of-Damocles feeling hanging over me. But now it's too late.

And, again, Beany knew something like thankfulness that there was another nail to pound out that old and rusty—yes, and festery—one of guilt. (But it wasn't *my* fault, she assured herself, for perhaps the four hundred and nine-teenth time.)

She began talking very fast to Kay as she guided Carlton's smooth-running car east toward the Veterans' Hospital. "Carlton said I could take his car to see the parade. So let's just load Elizabeth up and take her away from the hospital. It'd do her good—you know, as Faye said, there's no use her making herself sick, sitting out there. Oh, Kay, suppose they have to amputate. Let's just make her get away."

Kay didn't answer.

It was a long drive to the hospital, which was like a sprawling, listless town of ugly gray-white buildings, inhabited by civilian workers and sick men in maroon slacks and jackets; sicker men in gray-striped hospital robes; and very sick men with dull unseeing eyes, lying in beds. No wonder, Beany thought, Elizabeth looked so drained after her visits to Don. Could anything be more dismally depressing than a soldiers' hospital?

They went through three wards before they found Elizabeth. They knew by the nervous strain in her face, and by the empty bed near by, that Don was still in the operating room.

Elizabeth was playing cribbage with a soldier who was sitting on his bed in a limp, washed-out hospital robe. He was a young, snub-nosed soldier who had his right arm, from the elbow down, in splints so that only the tips of his swollen fingers could extract a card to play.

Elizabeth was dressed gaily in her old red suit and turquoise blouse, as though a bright exterior might pull her spirits up to match. Her new black hat framed her wan face and soft brown hair. Her eyes had the forced shine of eyes with tears pushing against the eyeballs. She smiled welcomingly at the girls and called out, "Just a minute, gals. I'm getting skunked in this cribbage game."

"Double-skunked," the victor smiled pleasedly.

The game finished, she came over to where a limping soldier placed chairs for them. Beany burst out, "Look, Elizabeth, I've got Carlton's car and if we hurry we can see the parade. We'll see Mary Fred—there'll just be tons of mums on the queen's float. You'll feel better it you get away from all this."

Elizabeth smiled into Beany's anxious eyes. "I couldn't,

Beany. I want to be here when Don comes out of the operating room. This is his bed here. They've got it ready, with
hot water bottles—and everything—for him. He's been in
a long time—" she had to steady her lips.

"But, Elizabeth, you'll just sit here and keep thinking
about it—about what the doctor said—that they might
have to—"

"They'll amputate to the knee if they find the bone
infected," Elizabeth said, as though she had already gone
over that fact with herself, and faced it. "But if Don comes
through all right, that doesn't matter. He'll still be
Don."

Beany could only stare at Elizabeth's set face. If only
she could think of something amusing to talk about so that
Elizabeth wouldn't keep watching the door into the hall,
down which a cart would come trundling. Beany groped
futilely about in her mind.

But Elizabeth was talking—talking almost feverishly as
though she would guard her young visitors from the forlorn
hospital life around them, yes, and even guard herself from
her own deep terror. And she had an interested, co-opera-
tive audience in Kay. Kay kept prodding her to tell of the
Malones and their growing up.

And finally Elizabeth was telling about when Beany was
a little girl and she, Elizabeth, sang in the choir. "I remember when we sang that 'Dona nobis pacem.' You see, Katherine, in church Latin we pronounce the c soft, so that it was
'pa-sem.' " She sang it softly, "Dona nobis—dona nobis—
pa-a -sem. And Beany thought we were singing, 'Don't
I know—don't I know—what pa-a said.' "

Kay joined Elizabeth in the chuckling memory.

Beany defended, "I never did know what pa said."

"It means 'Give us Thy peace,' Beany."

Beany edged forward on her chair. Why, that was what her father had said to her. "Give them peace, Beany. Give them happiness. Keep them from having trouble."

Elizabeth was saying, "But, of course, His peace doesn't mean a sit-down, folded-hands peace, or a running-away-from-trouble peace. He meant the kind of peace that comes of standing up to trouble—even taking it on the chin—"

"No," Beany contradicted her emphatically, as she had a sudden picture of Faye in her sea-green velvet hostess gown, serving her and Kay tea and tiny cream puffs. "No, that isn't peace. We've never had it. How could we when we—all of us—just go around sticking our necks out for trouble? I want us to have doors locked—and costumes for dancing and skating—and not always be churned up inside."

Elizabeth reached across and took Beany's hand. "Grown-ups have to be churned up inside. There's so much churning up along with growing up. There's a line I often think of—it didn't make sense to me when I read it a long time ago—but now it does. 'It is a terrible thing not to become a woman when one ceases to be a girl.' "

This time Kay edged forward on her chair. "What was it, Elizabeth? Say it again." She even repeated it soberly after Elizabeth said it, "—not to become a woman. . . when one ceases to be a girl." . . .

"It doesn't make sense to me," Beany said flatly.

Elizabeth said, "Oh, Beany, you blessed, maybe we've hurried you too fast into growing up. Maybe we haven't given you time to grow up easy. Is that it, Beany? Is that why you keep pulling back? But, honey, for every sorrow there's joy. 'The deeper sorrow carves into your being, the more joy you can contain.' My goodness, I'm a regular *Bartlett's Familiar Quotations* today."

"I don't believe all those silly quotations," Beany insisted stubbornly. "They're all lies—like that 'Parting is such sweet sorrow.' People just go on believing them. I think poets just wrote them to be writing."

"Poets wrote them out of their hearts," Elizabeth said, "out of their own suffering. It was their way of reaching out a hand to others and saying, 'I, too, have been there.'"

Before Beany could answer, the door of the operating room opened. A nurse hurried out, carrying a folded blanket. The three watched tensely, as she laid it on Don's empty bed, as she felt the hot-water bottle at the foot. Elizabeth's voice sounded frayed and thin, "Is it—over now?"

"Just about. The doctor will send him out in a minute."

Elizabeth's held-together features went slack, and her hands began plucking at her jacket buttons. She turned to the girls and said swiftly, "Beany, you know something I wish you two would do. You go on home and look after little Martie. I left him with Emerson, but he's quite a handful for the old fellow. He took to you so, Katherine. Beany, you'll have so much to do—with Mary Fred off in the parade—you'll have the cooking and all, but if I thought the little tike would be all right, I'd stay out here at the guest house tonight."

Kay said impulsively, "I'll stay with little Martie tonight and take care of him."

"Oh, Katherine, could you?" Again her lips twisted, righted into a too-bright smile. "Beany, tell her about the nightbirds that are *not* crying if he wants her to sing 'Red Wing.'"

The ward doors were flung open by an orderly. There was the bustle of nurses, the sound of rubber-tired cart wheels, and the wafted smell of anaesthetic. Elizabeth's agitation was terrible and piteous to see. But she hurriedly shepherded the two girls out, "You run along, kids—you run along and look after Martie and the old man."

Beany thought sickly as they left, She wants to get rid of us—of me. I've failed her. I wanted to save her. But she shunted me off—so as to save me.

And now they had to walk back through those three long wards. They had to slow their steps for men on crutches who walked ahead of them. They had to sidestep men in wheel chairs. They had to be the target for the eyes of men who lay on beds, with sometimes an arm, sometimes a leg, wrapped like a white cocoon.

Their footsteps became slow and hushed. For a new and unhappy soberness walked with them. A new humility that prodded at them and said, "The war isn't over for these men. For the rest of you, yes—but not for them. These are the ones who are still paying." More than humility, something of apology, even guilt. As though these sick and handicapped men were in themselves a reproach to anyone hurrying along on sound limbs, swinging unhampered arms—anyone rushing out into the sun and wind to glory in it. Beany said in a low voice to Kay, "I wonder if they feel bitter—"

Kay said softly, "I know. I wouldn't blame them if they hated us."

And then something happened. As Beany's and Kay's feet klopped softly on the maroon linoleum in the last ward, a loud and fervent wolf call sounded. It was as though a

window were opened, letting a swish of fresh air blow
through the fetid ward. Every man there sparkled and came
alive with appreciative twinkles and roguish grins.

That undulating, wolf-call whistle came from a young
man on a cot in a corner. He had a metal vise affair that
held his neck rigid. He looked like a small-town boy with
his rumpled straw-colored hair and reddish freckles and
engaging grin. He had taken a thermometer out of his
mouth, and he followed up the wolf call with a wave of it
and an exuberant, "Hiya Babes! If we'd known you were
coming, we'd've baked a cake."

Beany and Kay looked at each other and laughed spon-
taneously. They waved and called back, "We'll let you
know the next time."

They went on comforted, reassured by that bubbling-
over, unabashed, infectious zest for living. These boys were
just Anders and Dons and Johnnys. The wolf call and the
"Hiya Babes" had said better than any words the attitude
of American soldiers. "We can take it and go on from here.
We still like girls and fun. We're down, but far from out."

The two girls, without realizing it, were marveling at the
same thing over which all the nations of the world had
marveled. At the ability of "Yank" soldiers to wisecrack
through thick and thin. At that superabundance of humor
which was typical of American men and which carried them
through not only the thickness of tragedy, but through the
thin monotony of hospital days as well.

Silently, thoughtfully, Beany followed the big hospital
bus out of the grounds. It was dusk by the time they drove
down College Boulevard. Beany said, "Shouldn't we go
back to the Park Gate and tell Faye—or ask her if you can
stay all night to look after little Martie?"

For suddenly Beany, wearied by the emotional turmoil
of the day, longed for the eighth-floor haven of Faye's apartment. She longed for the hot fragrant tea and the cream
puffs. Just press a button and wait five minutes and there
was a waiter with a tray, asking, "Shall I set it here, ma'am?"
If you served tea in the Malone home you had to make it
yourself. (And find a marble in the sugar bowl.) But most
of all, Beany longed for Faye's untroubled, gay loveliness.
She longed to be reassured and refortified by it. Life at
the Malones was so scrambled and cluttered and full of
heart-twisting problems. Faye was like a bright, unshakable
star.

But Kay answered her resolutely, "No, I'll telephone
her from your house."

Then a queer thing happened. It happened just as Kay
was saying, "Oh, Beany, I might as well tell you. Maybe I'd
have gone on without realizing it exactly if it hadn't been
for Elizabeth. But today when she said, 'It is a terrible
thing not to become a woman when one ceases to be a
girl,'—why then—then I knew that Faye—"

Beany interrupted to say, "Speak of the angels, and you
hear the flapping of their wings. There's Faye, coming now
in her car—"

But it wasn't anything like a gentle flapping of angel's
wings. It was a swoosh and a zoom as the icecream-colored
car sped by them in reckless flight.

"She didn't even see us," Beany said disappointedly.

14

The Homecoming Dance

Old Emerson Worth had been knocked down by a hit-and-run driver.

Kay and Beany, after Beany had shakily parked Carlton Buell's car, walked into the gathering confusion in front of the Malone house. A knot of neighbors—all of them talking at once. A motorcycle policeman who came swerving up the street at the same time Beany and Kay had. A policeman in black puttees and a notebook with the pencil held under a wide elastic band. Johnny was there. Little Martie was there, half-crying and telling everyone, "He pushed me. I fell down—and hurted my knee."

And in the center of it all, taciturn and shaky, was old Emerson himself. Emerson was grumpily, almost ashamedly noncommittal about the whole event. Automatically, Beany rescued his white muffler from the street. Car wheels had muddied it; the wet fringe was chewed and torn.

"How did it happen?" everyone asked everyone else. Johnny told his version. He had driven home with the seven young rabbits he had picked up to use in his play and he was putting them in a box in the garage. All at once he had heard little Martie yell like a banshee—and he had come tearing out—

Mrs. No-complaint Adams gave her version. Now that she didn't give the Malones a half-day, she often stayed on at Judge Buell's to get their dinner. She had come to their front door to bring in the paper, and she had seen little Martie start across the street—and then she had seen Emerson Worth grab him. She guessed he must have shoved the little boy clear of the car. She guessed the old man—Mr. Worth, she called him with new respect—had lost his footing and fallen and been hit by the car.

"Did you get the license number of the car?" the policeman asked.

Land no, she hadn't thought about that. She had just started running to see how bad the old—Mr. Worth, she corrected, was hurt. But, come to think of it, it was one of those light-colored cars.

A driver of a bakery truck told his story. He had been down in the next block. He had been at the back of his truck getting out a sunshine cake, and he had seen the little fellow start across the street. He had seen the car driving down Barberry street at a fair clip—"Still and all, I don't see why the car couldn't have swerved out—or else stopped."

"Didn't the driver even slow down after he hit the man?" the policeman asked again.

"Slow down? Cripes, no, the car went so fast that, when it turned onto College, it took the corner on two wheels. I thought of following, but I knew this old crate of mine couldn't get within shooting distance. Yeh, it was a light-colored car all right."

Emerson Worth grew more testy at what he called "all this fool to-do." He glowered at Mrs. No-complaint Adams who wanted to make a hero out of him. And when an ambulance came clanging down the street and stopped, he waved his malacca cane irately and said, "Wasting the tax-payers' gas! Take it back until someone is hurt." Yes, he'd got hit in the head. It wasn't the first time his old dome had got smacked. Yes, he'd had the wind knocked out of him. But it wasn't the first time he'd had the wind knocked out of him, either. He had started out to the store, and he was going on to the store. He had promised Elizabeth he would get a piece of fresh salmon for supper.

"I'll get the salmon," Johnny promised. (Which he did, and brought home a chunk big enough to serve the whole Harkness football team.)

It was all Johnny and the police surgeon could manage to get Emerson into the house so that the surgeon could dress the wound on his head just under his ear. But first Emerson had to enjoin the officer, who closed his book and fitted his pencil under the tight rubber band, "Now don't you let a word of this get into the paper. I don't want Martie Malone reading about it and thinking he has to hightail it on home. You know who Martie Malone is?"

"Sure," the policeman had grinned. "And I'd hate to be the hit-and-run driver with Martie Malone, like a bloodhound on my trail."

"The driver's got to get me a new muffler—that's all I want out of it," Emerson grumbled, looking with angry eyes at the bedraggled muffler Beany still held. "But I don't want anything in the paper about this. Because I promised

Martie Malone to look after these kids while he's getting a rest in Arizona."

Beany's eyes rested on little Martie and the torn knee of his red corduroys, and she thought with choking gratitude, You did look after little Martie. Supposing you hadn't been there to give him a shove and send him sprawling—oh, supposing you hadn't!

Little Martie, with a three-year-old's capriciousness, had selected Kay to cling to. "My knee is hurted," he kept insisting aggrievedly.

"I'll put some salve on it and make it well," Kay soothed him absently.

Through all the questioning and the relating of sparse testimony Kay had listened with a tight sickness on her face. Her eyes turned from one to the other with a hunted, even wincing, fear. A question kept trembling on Beany's lips, "Kay, you don't think your mother. . . ?" But she couldn't ask it. . . . Oh, but that was silly, Beany reasoned with herself. Just because they had passed Faye on College Boulevard and Faye was clipping along at such a rate she hadn't seen them! Faye's car was light-colored. But they had passed other light-colored cars on College. Oh no, not Faye! Faye, in all her lilting young loveliness didn't belong in an ugly world of hit-and-run drivers.

Mrs. No-complaint Adams took the heavy package of fish out of Johnny's hands. "I'll make a drawn butter sauce for it," she said. In all their shaky concern, it gave a feeling of rightness to have Mrs. Adams take over the kitchen. She didn't go into explanations. Perhaps Emerson's saving of little Martie—her "little mister"—more than balanced the grievous injury of Emerson accusing her of making way with the lost silver spike. "If I'd known he never had any silver spike when he came here," she confided to Johnny, "I wouldn't have minded his muttering."

Emerson Worth was asleep by the time Mary Fred came home from the parade, wearing her navy-blue Chesterfield over the blue cloud of dress. Emerson's bolstering bluster was gone. The quieting tablet the surgeon gave him had taken effect and his bandaged head lay heavily on Martie Malone's pillow. A wispy, frail old man with hair like silken white floss.

Outside his door Johnny and Beany gave Mary Fred a whispered account of the accident and what the police surgeon had said. "This cut on his head isn't serious. But he's an old man. He'll suffer from shock—long-time shock. You'll have to expect it."

Mary Fred stood outside his door, her cheeks as brightly pink as a two-cent postage stamp from the wind and the excitement of the parade. From happiness? Beany wondered.

But Mary Fred shivered as she stood there in the puffed-sleeved, rippling-skirted glory of a freshman escort to the queen. "Let me out of this dress," she said and, reaching for the underarm zipper, gave it a vicious yank. "I loathe this dress! Beany, the queen made pleasant little chit-chat with all the attendants—but not with a lowly Independent. Not with the campus pariah."

Johnny asked, "Where's Lila? I thought she'd be coming on home with you. I got enough fish."

That was the thing that didn't seem right about Mary Fred's returning from the parade. Not to have Lila coming up the stairs with her, not to have Lila saying, "Johnny, you call mother and tell her I'm going to stay and eat with you."

Mary Fred said with thin brightness, "Lila went on to the buffet supper at the Delt house."

Beany asked troubledly, "Are you going to the Homecoming dance tonight, Mary Fred?"

"I don't want to go," Mary Fred said wearily. "I don't think I can face any more of this one-against-the-pack stuff."

"Did Ander ask you to go?"

Mary Fred laughed mirthlessly, "No, pet, I asked him. I had no maidenly reserve. I knew Ander wouldn't ask me because he had some sort of Sir Galahad idea about not involving me in his fight. . . . Beany, I'd have a good excuse not to go to the dance, wouldn't I? I could say Emerson had been hurt. I could say I wanted to go out to the hospital and stay with Elizabeth, couldn't I, Beany?"

"Of course, Mary Fred. Don't go—oh, don't go." They'll only hurt you more, Beany thought, if you go to the dance with Ander. The Delts would take that as an extra affront. They'll cold-shoulder you with added vengeance. Supposing not one of the frat fellows asked you to dance. I can't bear to think of you being a wallflower. Stay home, Mary Fred, so you won't be hurt any more.

As Beany walked down the stairs she heard Kay telephoning the Park Gate to tell her mother she would be staying overnight at the Malones to take care of little Martie.

Beany listened hopefully. If only Faye would say with her ready, rippling laugh, "Oh, did I pass you going down College? I was tearing like mad because of that appointment I had at the hairdresser's." Or maybe, "Don't you remember the dinner date I had, Kay—and I had to hurry and dress." And when Kay told her about Emerson being hurt,

she would say, "Oh, that's too bad! I wasn't off College at
all so I didn't even see it."

Beany stood beside Kay to ask, "Did she answer?"

"Ethel—she's the operator—said Faye gave word not to
ring her apartment because she has a headache."

"Won't she even ring if you tell her who you are?"

Kay shook her head, "No—Ethel said she wouldn't dare."

But Kay had another idea. She asked Ethel to connect
her with the Rhodes apartment and she talked to Norbett.
"Norbett, the operator won't ring Faye's—my mother's—
telephone. So could you go to her door and knock? She'll
surely answer that. Tell her I'm staying all night at the
Malones. Tell her—tell her—" Kay seemed to be choosing
her words carefully, "that the old man who stays with them
was hurt by a hit-and-run driver. Not seriously, tell her.
Tell her to be sure and telephone me. I'll be waiting."

The telephone rang while Kay was undressing little
Martie and promising to sing him "Red Wing" and also
"Old Black Joe." How much a part of Malone living was
wrapped about that silvery peal of the telephone! Kay slid
the little boy to his feet to answer it. But it was not Faye,
for Kay said, "Oh, Elizabeth!"

Four voices, Beany's, Johnny's, Mary Fred's, and Mrs.
No-complaint Adams' gave her a whispered admonition,
"Don't tell her about little Martie almost being hit."

Kay nodded understandingly, as she asked, "How did
the operation come out? . . . Oh, no—no, Elizabeth," she
said in a startled and shocked voice. But as she answered on,
the shock changed to one of marveling awe. "They did? . . .
Just imagine. . . . Oh, Elizabeth, you're so wonderful!" . . .

Each one was hesitant to put the question. They could only look entreatingly at Kay, as she slowly replaced the telephone. She answered their unspoken question then. "Yes—they had to amputate. But Elizabeth says it was very successful. She says she and Don are already making all sorts of plans. She says she's coming home in the morning after she sees Don again and make some cookies to take out to him—and for Johnny not to eat the nuts. She was laughing—Elizabeth was—and she said she was so happy. Because she had been so awfully afraid all day for fear the infection had spread and Don wouldn't pull through." Kay added reverently, "She didn't think it was a bit awful—the amputation, I mean."

They all stood there with tears rolling unashamedly down their cheeks. And yet they seemed to hear Elizabeth's soft laugh, to feel Elizabeth's relief, and gratitude, and elation that Don had come through it. And suddenly they knew, too, that what had happened wasn't awful at all. Elizabeth herself had said, "But it doesn't matter. He'll still be Don."

"The Malones are the beatenest," Mrs. No-complaint said, sniffling. "I've always told my family—the Malones can stand up to things that'd just flatten anybody else right out."

Beany said, "When we went out this afternoon she was playing cribbage—and letting the soldier skunk her."

For no reason that Beany could understand, Mary Fred said suddenly, "Mrs. Adams, if you're not using the teakettle, I'll give my hair a quick steam and stick it up in pin curls. Just look at it! And me going to the Homecoming dance tonight."

Beany couldn't get to sleep that night. The telephone
had rung intermittently all evening. When Emerson, old
newspaperman that he was, gave stern injunction to keep
"this piddling affair" out of the papers, he had never
thought of radio. A mention of the accident had been on
the evening newscasts. Everyone who knew Emerson Worth
or the Malones had telephoned, both to condole and to wax
indignant over the hit-and-run driver.

Not one of the telephone calls had been for Kay from
her mother at the Park Gate, though Norbett had reported
back to Kay that he had given the message to her mother.

Beany was still awake when Mary Fred came home. She
came into Beany's small room, and Beany turned on the
bed light which she had dimmed by pulling a blue anklet
over the bulb (because of Rosie and her family). Mary Fred
brought into the room the high-heeled excitement, the
bruised-corsage fragrance, of a sister coming home from
a dance.

She said, "It's bitter cold, Beany, and there's too much
fresh air on my sleeping porch for even my Girl Scout soul.
Can I climb in with you?"

It was like the old-time, giggly Mary Fred who wanted
to climb in and talk about the evening. She stepped out of
the rustling fluff of dress and said tenderly, "It's a love of
a dress, isn't it, Beany?"

Beany sat up, "Was it awful at the dance, Mary Fred?"

"The wind has changed, Beany."

"I know," Beany agreed impatiently. "The weather report says a cold wave. But what about the dance?"

"That's what I mean. The wind is tempering on the
campus. Or maybe it was that I didn't mind. I didn't,
Beany—honest. I kept thinking of sweet old Elizabeth tak-

ing it on the chin and going on from there. I kept thinking of Johnny telling about Emerson saying, 'So I got hit in the head. It isn't the first time my old dome has got smacked.' And so I went my own way—" She was humming softly as she pulled off her silver sandals.

Beany's mind filled in the words of the tune,

> *Oh, what a beautiful morning!*
> *Oh, what a beautiful day!*

Unlike Norbett, Mary Fred hummed it through to the end,

> *Everything's comin' my way.*

"Did you have *all* your dances?" Beany had to know.

"I did, indeed! I was no wallflower left to bloom alone. I danced with G.I.'s. Some of the frat fellows even made mistakes and danced with me. Ander didn't go begging for dances with the gals either. He was just too Gene Autrey for them to pass up. . . . Hey, where are your knit bedsocks? My feet are like frozen perch fillets. . . . Beany, the queen had chit-chat with me. Just old buddy-buddy."

In her striped butcher-boy pajamas Mary Fred snuggled in beside Beany. Beany pulled out the light and squirmed down blissfully. Now I can sleep. The queen talked to Mary Fred. Surely the Delts are relenting. Surely she'll get her bid yet. And then she won't be left out when they have buffet suppers.

In the darkness Mary Fred said, "Do you know what started the wind blowing the other way on the campus? It was that letter in the *Call* by a Lover of Justice. He gave them all pause. He blew the cobwebs off tradition. Who do you suppose it was, Beany?"

"I don't know. Do you suppose it could have been Father?"

"No—I don't think so. No—I'm sure it wasn't."

Maybe it was because Beany, in thinking of that article, thought of Norbett Rhodes thrusting the paper at her that day in typing. Of course it was all over between her and Norbett! But in Beany's stage of peace and joy over Mary Fred, any happiness seemed possible—even Norbett's old way of turning to her and asking, "Beany, what is two of in *occasion?*"

She reached stealthily for her jar of freckle cream. She knew by heart the directions which ended, "Best results are obtained by night application. $1.25."

15

Kathleen Mavourneen

Beany sat up in bed the next morning beside the soundly sleeping Mary Fred and sniffed as diligently and excitedly as a rat terrier. She sniffed, and her eyes widened. It was the smell of a pipe that sifted through the house like incense. Surely no other pipe but the one Martie Malone cleaned with a broom straw and tamped tobacco in so lovingly had that heartening, warming fragrance; more than fragrance, a sort of "God's in his heaven, all's right with the world" assurance.

Beany slid swiftly out of bed and into her clothes. She closed the door softly behind her. As though any kind of door-closing would waken Mary Fred! Beany took the stairs, à la Johnny, two steps at a time. For, added to the pipe fragrance, she heard the unmistakable song telling Kathleen Mavourneen that the gray dawn was breaking.

Martie Malone was home again.

His enfolding arms caught Beany at the kitchen door.

One of her braids snagged on the button of his tweed vest the way it always did. Martie gave her braid an extra tug as he loosened it, said, "Beany, blessed," the way he always did.

Her eyes feasted on the deep tan of his face. The tired sag had given way to the network of laugh wrinkles around his eyes. Beany remembered thinking once that you could almost play tit-tat-toe on those smile wrinkles of his. She reported soberly, "I tried to look after the family—but I didn't get very far."

He laughed heartily at that. "Feed them, love them, say a prayer—and what else can we do with a family like ours, Beany?"

"But how did you know about Emerson? I mean, is that why you came home?" she asked.

"I heard it over the radio. Maybe I was just glad of an excuse to get back home and into harness. I heard it on the eight-o'clock broadcast, so I threw my things in my bag— Beany, don't scold me too much for the way I packed!— and caught a plane out at midnight."

"How is Emerson this morning?" Beany asked Johnny as he joined them.

"Very tractable. And, after all his warning us not to send for Father, awfully glad to see him. He's asleep again after his morning coffee. I had to pretend his pills were aspirin to get them down him. The doctor told us to keep him quiet."

Johnny had made coffee. He had made it in their biggest company coffeepot. But, as it happened, many people sifted in that stormy Saturday morning to sit at the round kitchen table and hear Johnny ask, "Sugar? Cream? Or both?"

Kay was cooking the oatmeal while little Martie waited in his high chair. Little Martie's halo of golden curls was still untouched. "No shearing till after the play," Johnny had passed verdict.

Johnny had to show Kay how to salt the water and bring it to a boil before she added the oatmeal. "Don't let *him* measure it for you," Beany cautioned, "or you'll have enough for all Barberry street."

Martie Malone smiled at Kay. "Pretty nice to have a friend of Beany's come in and give us a hand." Perhaps he hoped to lighten the tight look on Kay's face.

But Kay's face had worn that tight and wincing fear ever since the accident. Instead of relaxing, it grew tighter as the morning passed.

The motorcycle policeman who had come to the scene of the accident yesterday came again. He sat and stirred two spoonfuls of sugar into his cup of coffee, his ruddy face intent with anxiety to prove to Martie Malone that he wasn't passing up any opportunity to find the hit-and-run driver.

And still another sat down and had a cup of Johnny's coffee. The driver of the bakery truck. He had a clue which the policeman jotted down in his battered notebook. "I just figured it out that that car that hit the old fellow turned off Barberry; it must have gone past Mac's garage and filling station up on College then."

So the driver of the bakery truck had asked Mac, and sure enough, Mac had seen the light-colored car. He remembered it because he was out at the curb taking off a tire, and this car went zooming by like a bat out of Hades, and splashed muddy slush all over his clean overalls. A woman was driving it. Mac remembered that the license number had three sixes in it. Yeh, and he was pretty sure it was an Oldsmobile.

The motorcycle policeman stood up. Light Olds, woman driver, three sixes in the license number. Well, that gave them something to work on.

He had to step around Kay who was at the telephone in the hall. This time Kay was so grimly insistent that Ethel rang her mother's apartment. Beany finally heard Kay say, "Faye, I want to tell you the old man—the one that was knocked down by the hit-and-run driver—isn't hurt bad. Martie Malone came home early this morning—" . . . But Kay was just telling her mother the happenings at the Malones, wasn't she? . . . "They think they have clues to trace the driver. Faye, don't you think you'd better come over? Faye, you've *got* to come!"

And still another caller sounded the knocker on the Malone front door. Maybe this was Faye.

But it was Norbett Rhodes, his thin face blue with the cold. He stood tense and uncertain outside the threshold. He spoke with disjointed awkwardness. "The *Tribune* sent me out. They want a story on the accident you had. I tried to tell them —I tried to talk them into sending somebody else. I didn't want—to come butting in—"

Part of Beany wanted to cry out, "You're not butting in. Come in, Norbett, and warm youself by the fire in our fireplace. I'll give you coffee and cinnamon rolls. Don't act as though this is a hateful chore for you."

But how could a girl say that to the fellow who had once been crazy about her sister and been jilted by her, who had declared himself the Malone enemy? "It's war to the hilt," he had flung at her.

But Johnny could say it. Johnny, as Miss Hewlitt said,

had malice toward none. Johnny's own heart was big as the world and yet had no space in it for memory grudges. Johnny came through the hall, carrying wood for the fireplace.

He smiled at Norbett over the pine chunks. "Hey, Norb, come on in the living room. Wait till I put this wood on the fire and I'll get you a cup of coffee. I want to talk to you about the play. Emerson's accident sure left me in a hole, and I wondered if you'd help me out."

"He came for the *Tribune*," Beany said awkwardly. "He came to get a story on Emerson's accident."

"We'll fix you up with that, too," Johnny said, hunkering down to feed the fire in the huge fireplace. With no awkwardness at all, Johnny included his father in the conversation. "Father got in this morning. That's why the roaring fire. Got to keep these thin-blooded Arizonians warm. Do you know Father, Norbett?"

"Just *of* him," Norbett said, desperately trying to be at ease as Martie Malone shook hands with him.

"Better hotten up the coffee for Norbett, Beany," Johnny said.

Beany turned the flame high under the coffee percolator. She used one of their best china cups. She picked out the cinnamon roll with the thickest icing.

As she put the plate in Norbett's hands, Johnny was telling him about Emerson. "He isn't hurt seriously, yet we can't count on him to handle the narrator part in the play. But we're going to coddle him like everything so he'll be able to go and *see* it. That would really give him a build-up. Poor old codger. So I wondered if you'd take over either the lighting or the narrator part, Norbett. You can take your choice. Carlton Buell offered to handle the lighting and let me take the narrator, but Carlton doesn't have the feel of theater the way you do. Gosh, if you could manage to give us a hand—"

There's the olive branch, Norbett, Beany was thinking. Reach out and take it—please, reach out and take it!

But Norbett only looked at Johnny without answering. He only twisted the pink-flowered cup in his cold, uncertain fingers.

"Well, think it over," Johnny said, "and see if you can squeak it in with your reporting and making up chem. Oh, hurray, there's Elizabeth coming in. Wait here till I go talk to her. Was there some coffee left, Beany?"

"Yes, lots," Beany said.

And suddenly Beany and Norbett were alone in the Malone living room in front of the crackling fire. She could hear her father, and Johnny, and little Martie besieging Elizabeth with loving greetings and questions. The rattle of the coffeepot, the slam of the breadbox, and over it all little Martie yelling delightedly, "She sang me about a duck."

Norbett got to his feet. Beany took the plate from him. "Beany," he said, looking hard at the fire, "I want to tell you something. I've always thought Johnny was tops. Maybe you won't believe it, but I have. I've always wished I could be like him. I wish I could work with him on his play but—"

"But you can. He wants you to."

He didn't answer that. "I'd give anything I've got if I could undo . . . I mean I've done him a skunky trick. You remember what I wrote you after my car was impounded—that 'Revenge is sweet'?"

"Yes, I remember. You said you'd never rest easy till you rubbed Malone noses in the dirt."

"That's it. That's what I tried to do. I wish I'd known all that revenge quotation before I believed it."

"What is it?"

" 'Revenge is sweeter than life—so think fools.' "

The clack of the door knocker interrupted. Beany's father called from the hall, "Catch it, Beany. Must be a friend of yours—or Mary Fred's. It's a girl."

Faye Maffley stood at the door when Beany opened it. A girl, her father had said, when he had caught a glimpse of the taffy-colored hair and the Kelly green suit under the short fur jacket. Beany's delighted eyes took in the lovely perfection of her. Green gloves to match the suit. A big green suede pouch bag to match the gloves. Beany had seen Kay wear the twin outfit to this.

Beany knew a great surge of relief at sight of her—yes, and self-reproach that in her own mind she had even connected Faye with the cowardly hit-and-run driver. For here stood Faye, utterly unruffled, carefree, and radiant. Here was Faye, ready to win over the rest of the Malone family to her creed.

Beany, flushing with happy pride, ushered her into the living room and introduced her to her father, Elizabeth, Johnny. . . . Don't you see how glowing and lovely she is? She's discovered the fountain of youth, and I kept trying to show it to all of you. She knows how to be happy. Faye never sticks her neck out for trouble. Please notice, all of you. You'd never dream she was old enough to be Kay's mother, would you? . . .

It even angered Beany that everyone didn't fall under the

spell of Faye's girlish smiles, of Faye's saying archly, "I've heard so much about Martie Malone." Why should Norbett stand braced tensely? Why should Kay say, "You were so long coming," with cold accusation.

Faye turned with a dazzling smile to Martie Malone. "I've come to confess and throw myself on your mercy. And I'm frightened half to death of you." Yet her confident smile was that of a small child who has only a small and easily forgivable misdemeanor to admit. "I—well, I was thinking of Kay when I drove on—and after all, I could see that I hadn't hurt him."

Beany turned her amazed eyes to her father. Yet Martie Malone didn't look surprised. "Go on, Mrs. Maffley," he said.

"Oh, call me Faye—no one ever calls me *Mrs.* Maffley. It's always just Faye and Kay. Well, as I was saying, I was driving down your street yesterday—and it all happened so suddenly—you know how those things do. Really, the old man stepped right in front of my car."

She looked appealingly about at the shocked faces. No one spoke until Martie Malone said levelly, "But you knew it after you hit him, Mrs. Maffley. You must have seen in your mirror that you knocked him down, even if you didn't feel the jolt, which you probably did. And yet you turned the corner and raced up College. I was talking on the phone to Mac and he said you were going by his place pretty fast—like a bat out of Hades, he put it—and that's three blocks up College."

Faye was twisting the Kelly green gloves in her hand, as though she had not expected such stern judgement. But again she smiled with winning appeal into Martie Malone's unsmiling eyes. "Oh, I know I shouldn't have kept on. I started to stop. Honest and truly I did. And then I thought of Kay—I couldn't bear to think of all the ugly publicity for Kay. I—well, I guess I was afraid. But then I decided I'd come and make a clean breast to you because Beany's always told me how wonderfully—understanding you are." Her dazzling smile came out again.

Beany squirmed, as an inexplicable feeling of revulsion went through her at Faye's coquetry. Could Johnny be right? Was there something gruesome about a woman Faye's age affecting such naïve childishness?

Faye added, "I decided to trust to your understanding and leniency."

"I'm afraid leniency—as you call it—isn't in my hands any longer," Beany's father said quietly.

Beany looked across at Kay. Why, Kay had reverted back to the girl Harkness High called Frozen-face. Frozen-face sitting there on the window seat, holding little Martie and buttoning and unbuttoning the strap on his corduroy overalls. Beany slid up close to her. Johnny took this moment to angle a piece of wood on to the fire, and under cover of his clinking at it with the poker, Beany whispered, "Kay, you knew? How did you know it was Faye?"

Kay answered lifelessly, "I noticed when she passed that one of her lights was cracked. I always look at her lights, because she's always bumping into something and breaking them."

Faye was still all helpless, ingratiating, pleading. "You mean then that you won't help me? That you'll let the police go ahead and—and impound my car?"

"I'm sorry, but I don't think you have any business driving a car. A car isn't a toy, you know. You were right when you said the old man stepped in front of you. If he hadn't, you'd have hit the little boy. I don't see how you missed seeing him. The next time a child runs across the street in front of you, there mightn't be an old man to risk his life and grab him back."

"But there'll be publicity. You're a newspaperman—you know how the papers build up things like that."

"Yes, I know," he said gently, but inexorably. "Yet if it were my own son or daughter, accused of running away from an accident, I'd feel they deserved whatever they got."

And then suddenly, even as Beany's eyes were on Faye's face, all the coy and smiling appeal went out of it. It wasn't a young face, nor a happy one; it was sharp and vicious. Her voice wasn't a young, lilting voice; it was shrill and spiteful. "Is that so? Well, it is *your son* that I'm accusing of running away from an accident. Maybe you won't be so high-minded about it now. Maybe you'll change your mind about covering up this traffic violation of mine. Maybe you won't think it's so nice for Martie Malone's son to get publicity after all your fine talk about reckless driving."

"My son?" Martie Malone challenged.

And Johnny turned away from the fire to stare stupidly and speechlessly at her.

Norbett said savagely, "Now look, Mrs. Maffley, I told you you'd better forget that."

"Why should I?" she said, with a malicious laugh. "I can prove that Johnny Malone was driving a car that collided with me one night and that he didn't even have a brake and light sticker on his car."

Faye was pulling apart the drawstrings of her beautiful green suede bag. She drew an object from it and held it up with dramatic triumph. If a gun had suddenly been pointed at Beany's ribs, her heart couldn't have thudded any slower or harder than it did now under her ribs, her sweater, and her cellophane apron.

"Here's the door handle off your son's car. It came off the night he collided with me," Faye said with vindictive heat. "It was on my car between my lights and the hood when I got back to the garage. The minute Norbett saw it, he said it was off Johnny Malone's car."

16

Mrs. *Maffley*

Maybe it was only a minute, though it seemed to Beany, perched there on the window seat beside the expressionless Kay, an eternity that the battered door handle held all eyes like a magnet. There was still a feathery fleck of blue on it, left from Johnny's paint job of last summer. Beany sat appalled and stunned, and yet part of her mind was thinking irrelevantly, "We could have used steel wool to take that dab of paint off," and another part of her mind reminded her, "You always knew that door handle would show up somehow, some place."

There was such a pounding in her ears that voices had a blurred, faraway sound. Johnny's petrified voice did. *"I collided with you! When?"*

So did Norbett's harshly unhappy one. Norbett was shrinking back against the mantel—(it'd be awful if he scorched his pants' leg!)—and his face looked younger and thinner with shame. "Yes, I told her it was the door handle to Johnny's car. That was just when I was laying for you Malones, hoping I could get something on any of you. Faye—Mrs. Maffley—came to my uncle's dinner party and she said she was late because a car had bumped into her and smashed her lights. A couple of days later she showed me the doorhandle. And I told her whose it was."

Beany swallowed hard. The time is now, the time is now, as some radio refrain put it.

But she was thankful for even the very respite she was granted by Elizabeth's saying matter-of-factly to Kay, "Katherine, don't let Martie squirm on your lap and get your skirt all rumpled. Come over here, pieface."

And then Beany heard her own voice say—she had meant it to be vigorously strong, but it came out thin and wispy, "It was Johnny's car all right, but he wasn't driving it. I was. But I didn't collide with her. I was driving home on College and all at once a car hit me. I didn't know whose car it was, because when I got out the car was gone."

There, it was out! No, not quite. She knew what the next question would be. She knew who would ask it. So she tumbled out the answer to it before her father could ask, "Why didn't you report it, Beany?" "I knew I should report it. But I was scared—and I was ashamed, too. I knew when I took Johnny's car, I shouldn't—but I was in such a hurry to get hold of Norbett before he left the chem lab at Harkness. I wanted him to do something about the write-up about Ander. I drove over to school to ask him. I was coming home when— But the other car hit me."

Faye's laugh was airily belittling. "Of course she'd deny that it was her fault."

Beany felt something give in her. A star had turned to tinseled dust in her heart—a star that she had thought an unshakable bright beacon. For now a mournful dirge in her was saying, "Faye is a liar. Faye is a coward." She even had the acrid taste of dust in her mouth.

Norbett said tersely, "Beany doesn't lie."

"After all," Faye said with the same sure smile, "it's just her word against two of us. For Kay was with me. Kay will agree with me."

Beany's sick eyes groped for Kay's. But Kay's eyes were fixed on the lowest black tip of the poker standing by the fireplace. Mrs. Maffley's eyes kept probing at Kay; her voice, edged with warning and threat, repeated, "Kay will agree with me, won't you Kay?"

Everyone waited for Kay to speak—Kay, who sat there like a blond statue of a girl in a yellow sweater. Oh, what would Frozen-face say about the time she was riding with Faye in the ice-cream wagon that snowy night?

Elizabeth prodded her gently, "Tell us, Katherine."

And Kay's voice had a frozen indifference, when she said without looking up, "It was just the way Beany said. Faye didn't see the stop sign. It was snowing, but she always misses stop signs unless I tell her. She ought to wear glasses but she says glasses make her look like the librarian back in Upton, Utah. She was hurrying because it had taken her so long at the beauty parlor and she was late to the Rhodes' dinner party."

So that's that, her voice seemed to say.

Norbett broke the grating silence. "Give him back the door handle, Faye. He's been hunting all over to find one that would fit his car door." Norbett took it out of Faye's lax hand. He handed it to Johnny, said, "Here you are," as though he were saying, "Here, Johnny, I could kick myself for telling her." . . . And Johnny said, "Well, I'm glad to

get that antique back." As though he were saying, "Well,
just forget about it, Norb."

Faye stood there irresolutely in her costume suit of Kelly
green, with the green quill feather like a crooked exclama-
tion point stuck through her little hat. But the taffy-colored
hair framed a face that went incongruously with that rippling, sixteen-year-old hair-do. Her face was like the face
of a doll which had been left out in harsh weather and
looks bleached and lumpy and lacking. Beany thought, she
isn't pretty. I thought she was, but she isn't. Elizabeth looks
so tired and her eyes are so heavy, but she's not drained
inside. There's an inside shine to her.

And out of the very dust that the fallen star left in Beany's
heart, there began to be erected a new and solider founda-
tion. What was it Elizabeth had said—"not a running-
away peace, but the peace that comes of taking it on the
chin." That was Elizabeth's peace.

Faye pulled her fur jacket closer, with a tinny jangle of
charm bracelet. "I've got a wretched headache. We'd better
go home, Kay."

Kay announced in that same cold uncaring voice, "I'm
not going home."

Martie Malone reproached mildly, "Kay, she's your
mother."

Kay jerked to her feet. Even as Elizabeth had predicted,
her skirt was mussed from little Martie's squirmings, but
she didn't bother to smooth it or to straighten it so that the
kick pleat would be in front. There was nothing frozen
about her face or her voice now. "She cheated me out of
having a mother," she flung out thickly. "She had to be a
chum to me. She made me feel sorry for her because she
said she never had any girlhood. Well, she can't keep on

being a girl forever, can she? I can't keep on being sixteen
—being a doll for her to dress up and make dancing dresses
and skating outfits for. I want friends of my own age, but she
won't let me chum with anyone but her. If I make a friend,
she packs up and moves on. We left Colorado Springs because I was fool enough to make a girl friend there. I was
afraid to be friends with Beany because I knew—I knew so
well what it would mean."

Perhaps it was Martie Malone, perhaps it was Elizabeth,
who tried to put in a steadying word, but a dam had burst
inside Kay, whom her father called Katherine, and she
couldn't be stopped. "I won't go home. It isn't a home—it's
just a playhouse. I won't go on running away from everything that isn't pretty and ruffly and sweet. Please let me
stay here with you until I can write Father and ask him if I
can go back to Utah with him. Please let me—" And then
she was sobbing, brokenly, convulsively.

She was sobbing, and when Faye took a step toward her,
she screamed out, "Don't you touch me!" It was Beany's
arms she sought refuge in.

A cold, sobering thought thrust deep into Beany. This is
tragedy. . . . Mrs. No-complaint Adams often said, "Oh,
it's tragic that your mother had to die and leave you." But
they still had a hundred memories to warm them. Even
Lila, for all her resenting her mother's bossing, would turn
to her capable arms when sobs racked her. . . . Outside
happenings weren't tragedies. Not Mary Fred's cold-
shouldering by the Delts. If time went against Johnny, and
Emerson didn't ever see his book in print—or even see the
events come alive on the stage—well, then Johnny would
have to say, "I tried so hard for the old fellow," but he'd be
right inside. Not even a soldier having to learn to walk with

an artificial leg was tragic—not if the one he loved walked
in step beside him. Why no, it was inside feelings that made
tragedy when they were wrong. If someone you loved let
you down. Or—as Beany looked at Faye's empty face—
knowing you had let someone you loved down.

Kay's mother stood there, startled and arrested by Kay's
vehement, "Don't you touch me!" She looked about her
helplessly, even pitiably, as though in this moment she was
realizing, "It is a terrible thing not to become a woman
when one ceases to be a girl." And a terrible thing not to be
a mother when your daughter needs a mother.

And then something happened that broke the sick, em-
barrassed tension. One of Rosie's pups came waddling into
the room—the brown one Kay had named Pierre. He
rushed for Johnny's pants' leg and grabbed it with a lion-
sized growl, and braced himself while he tugged and shook
it. Little Martie, desperate at Kay's grief, yanked the puppy
loose from its hold, scooped it up and poked it into her
arms. "Here," he said urgently, "Here, you can have it."

"It's your pup, Katherine," Elizabeth said. "I guess he
thinks it's time you took him home."

Martie Malone said, "I guess she could take the little
dog home with her, couldn't she, Mrs. Maffley?"

It might have been the emphasis Martie Malone put on
the *Mrs.* Maffley. For it seemed to Beany, watching her
over Kay's shoulder, that some of her empty girlishness
sloughed off and she tried to stretch to the stature of a *Mrs.*
Maffley, Kay Maffley's *mother.* For she answered in a sort
of resigned mother's voice that seems to say, "Dear, dear!
what we mothers have to put up with!", "Well, I guess so—
if Kay thinks she can take care of it. If you think it's old
enough to eat by itself—and—and—"

"You can put papers down for him at first," Beany hastened to say. "And he can eat. They're already drinking canned milk with a little warm water in it. And we'll tell Kay how to cook hamburger and carrots and oatmeal together."(Those peach-colored curtains in the playhouse kitchen wouldn't look so rose-petal fresh with a stewpan steaming daily beneath them. But a kitchen was the heart of a home and its curtains had no right looking like store-window curtains.)

Mrs. Maffley said, "You can take the pup home, Kay. And then—then when we go back to Utah in the spring, we can take him with us."

Oh, Kay, did you hear that?—Beany wanted to cry out. She'll go back to the little town even if it does make her hair dingy, even if there isn't any laundry service. Kay's sobs slackened. She had heard.

She turned and smiled a little wabbly smile at her mother. "I'll have to put him under my coat, so he won't get snowed on." she said.

"If you need any help, Kay, just call on me. I can drop in and show you how to fix his goulash," Johnny said.

"I'll take care of him while Kay is in school," Mrs. Maffley promised.

. . . Yes, Beany thought, she could almost see what Mrs. Maffley would be like when she put up the taffy-colored hair, when maybe she'd say, "Kay, did you see where I put my glasses?" . . .

Kay, holding the little brown dog in her arms and laughing chokily when it licked her chin, started out of the room with her mother. It was Mrs. Maffley who humbly pulled Kay's coat together over the little dog as Johnny opened the door for them and they stepped out into the snow.

And, as they went down the front steps, it didn't seem like a winsome twosome—or, as Johnny said, a gruesome twosome—but as though a mother and daughter had gone out together.

17

Pink Ice Cream

Mary Fred had slept through the whole morning. Even though Father had taken her up a cup of coffee and had sat on her bed talking, even though Mary Fred had said then, "Oh, glory be, I didn't know it was so late. I'm going to get right up," she didn't. She had dallied a minute too long on the pillow.

It was almost noon when a special delivery letter came for Mary Fred Malone and Beany signed for it and took it up to her and yelled out, "Mary Fred, wake up! 'The snail's at the morn.' "

Mary Fred sat up, opened eyes that seemed glued together, stretched with such abandon that the top button almost popped off her striped pajamas. "It's the *lark* that's at the morn—and the *snail* that's on the thorn, if I remember correctly," she said thickly.

"Well, anyway it's noon. And here's a letter for you. It came special. You'd better pull this sweater over your shoulders. It's bitter cold out."

Beany stood there, a little surprised that she didn't *look* different to Mary Fred. Because she *felt* so different. No more albatross—only it was that missing door handle!—around her neck. And she was growing up.

But Mary Fred only took the letter, held it while she yawned luxuriously once more, and pushed her disheveled hair back from her sleep-flushed face. She took a minute to ask, "Um-mm! Who's cooking what? Smells heavenly."

"Elizabeth is making brownies to take out to Don. Father's going out with her. Mrs. No-complaint just arrived and she's making chile. Mary Fred," Beany added shyly, "Norbett came—and he's still here."

"Norbett? What's the big attraction—you?"

Don't I wish I was, Beany thought wistfully. Maybe he's just hanging around, waiting till Mary Fred comes downstairs.

Beany said, "Johnny and he are going great guns on the play. Norbett is taking over the lighting, and Johnny, the narrator part."

"Imagine Norbett taking a backstage part! Old big-shot Norbett! Old show-off Norbett!"

"He isn't big-shot Norbett," Beany flared. "He isn't show-off Norbett."

"Okay, toots, okay—if that's the way you feel. He's shrinking-violet Norbett." And then her voice softened, "Norbett's all right, Catherine Cecilia. Don't mind me. Beany, give me a bobby pin out of your braids to open my letter."

The envelope which Mary Fred turned over was almost square and of heavy white paper such as wedding invitations come in. Mary Fred slid the bobby pin under the deep V-shaped flap. She unfolded the thick double sheet with a

crest at the top. Beany edged closer on the bed to read it.
Why, it was from the Delts! " . . . the honor to invite
you . . . . . pledging on December seventh. . ."

Beany breathed out, "Mary Fred, it's your bid! Your bid
from the Delts! They did change their mind. They sent
it special so you'd get it today."

Mary Fred turned the letter over in her hand. She only
grunted a little sadly, "H'mmm!" Slowly she folded it and
put it back in the stiff white envelope, glancing absently
at the smooth, girlish writing on it which had run a little
from the wet snow, and at the array of stamps. She said with
a half-smile, "If this had come a week ago—even yesterday—it would have seemed the most precious thing in the
world to me—the open Sesame—"

"Doesn't it now, Mary Fred?" Beany asked earnestly.

"It's too late," Mary Fred said, shaking her head. "Not
very much too late—just a little bit. What they put me
through," she sighed, as her memory turned back, "Lord
save us, what they put me through! The days I'd have gone
running to eat out of their hand if they had even reached it
out to me. The nightmares I've had. Funny, isn't it, Beany,
how you care so hard—and then, somehow, you stop
caring. Funny, how I wanted this so hard—and then, when
I stopped wanting it, it came. I stopped wanting to belong
last night. And I guess it was last night that they decided
I'd do after all—maverick though I am."

"But, Mary Fred, the Delts are in everything—and you'd
be in the swim."

"Old die-hard Beany!" Mary Fred said fondly. "Look,
puddin'-head, I'll be in—in my own way—without them.
I'll make the friends I want to make. Maybe some of them

will be Delts—sweet old Lila will always be my chum. No, I'm not scared now of going it alone."

She threw the covers back and the heavy envelope slid to the floor with a small plop. One of Rosie's pups came sniffing at it, back arched, pretending it was a dread enemy. "You know, Beany, I even owe the Delts a debt. Until they pushed me out on my own, I didn't know I could go it alone. I might have gone on thinking I had to run with the herd if all this hadn't happened."

She was looking out the window through the white curtain of snow toward the red brick house of Mrs. Socially-prominent Adams. "How deep is the snow, anyway? Ander and I were going out to the stables to see my Mr. Chips and his Mike. They're both getting so fat and sassy we decided to run some of it out of them. Did Ander call me?"

"Yes, he called and said to let you sleep."

"Ander called," Mary Fred giggled through her red sweater as she pulled it on over her head. Two more synchronized movements and she was zipping up her plaid skirt. "Well, thank heaven, I don't have to go running after Ander now. Thank heaven, Ander won't go bolting for the tall timber every time he sees me."

"Like a rope-shy bronc," Beany giggled with her.

They were still giggling when Johnny stuck his head in the door. "Guess what?" he asked.

"What?"

"They never did find the silver spike."

"So I've heard tell," Mary Fred said.

"You see all these miners came down from Georgetown, bringing a silver spike—"

"I know, I know," Beany said. "And the governor was to pound it in for the last spike on the railroad, and while he was making a speech, all these miners began hunting through their pockets in frenzy—but no silver spike. Then what?"

Johnny leaned in the doorway and laughed heartily. "Historical records are divided on whether it was a silver spike that was pounded in or not. But old Emerson remembers what happened. He says a whack on the head is good for the memory. He says that these fellows were celebrating the night before—"

"Skip all that," Beany said impatiently. "Does the railroad have the last spike or not?"

"It has *a* spike. Emerson says somebody just picked up an ordinary spike and wrapped it in paper and handed it to the governor and he pounded it in and everybody thought it was a silver spike."

"Does this story have a moral?" Mary Fred demanded.

"Moral? I wasn't thinking of a moral. I just thought you'd both rest easier if you knew about it. But if you must have a moral you could drag one in by the hind legs and reason thusly; any old spike is as good as a silver spike if you just think it's a silver spike."

"Oh, Johnny," Beany said exasperatedly. "Please—let it lay. . . . Did you feed all those rabbits you gathered up to play leading roles in your play?"

"The rabbits, my turtle dove, have dined on the head of lettuce we had in the icebox and a package of corn flakes. Also some burned toast in case they need carbon in their diet. What did you feed Frank when he was at a tender age?"

"Rolled barley. All rabbits need rolled barley."

Johnny ran his fingers through his long, wavy black

thatch of hair. "Norbett," he yelled, "we've got to get rolled barley for the rabbits. Beany says so. Only—I'd like to get busy on that final scene so you could give it the once-over."

And that was how it happened that Beany and Norbett walked through the snow toward the store that was a feed store in winter and an ice station in summer. That was how it happened that Beany, who didn't like rabbits, was walking seven blocks through the snow to bring home rolled barley for seven of them.

The snow sifted down as gently as torn paper. "A blue light on the stage for snow," Norbett mused. Red frolicked along beside them, flipping his wet tail on Beany's legs. A feeling of just-rightness walked with Beany as she matched her steps to Norbett's. Well, almost just-rightness. She wished Johnny hadn't bellowed out, "Norbett, why don't you go with Beany and get the barley?" She wished she didn't keep wondering if Norbett was waiting around till Mary Fred came downstairs.

They came to Downey's drugstore and stood in its door-way to whack the snow off their shoulders. Beany took off her crusted green wool scarf and shook it, then tied it on again. Well, if it was Mary Fred Norbett wanted to know about, she'd tell him.

"Norbett, Mary Fred got a bid from the Delts. But she isn't going to pledge."

"Isn't she?" Was he just pretending he didn't care whether Mary Fred pledged or not? "Well, I'm glad she got a chance to turn them down."

"We were talking last night about the wind changing on the campus. Mary Fred says it was that letter—that 'Lover of Justice' letter that sort of jolted them out of their smugness over that tradition stuff. It blew the cobwebs out, she said."

"So!" Norbett said. "Did you ever find out who wrote it?"

"No. We wondered and wondered who did. I thought maybe Father might have, but Mary Fred said no, she was sure he hadn't. We haven't thought to ask him."

He said impatiently, "Beany, I'd think a newspaper-man's daughter would be more alert to style in writing. Of course the copy editor corrected the misspelled words in it."

Her fingers, fumbling at the knot that wouldn't stay knotted under her chin, stopped. "Norbett—you wrote it! Norbett, why didn't you tell me?" . . . But maybe he thought I'd guess it that day in typing when he shoved it under my nose. That day I couldn't even fight with him because my eyes were all red from crying. . .

"Why didn't you give me a chance?" he answered her back. "You wouldn't even look at me for sitting there, typing away on that stuff about not failing if you don't limit your endeavor."

"You wrote it, Norbett! And that was what helped Mary Fred." And then she had to ask it. Even though she was afraid to hear the answer, she had to ask it. "Did you write it to make it up to Mary Fred? I mean because you wanted to make it easier for her on the campus? Or so Mary Fred would like you better?"

He reached out and his impatient fingers tied the knot under her square chin. He said gruffly, "Stop always think-ing I'm eating my heart out for Mary Fred. Do you know what?"

"What?"

"There's something lacking about Mary Fred now that I know you."

"Lacking about Mary Fred? What?"

"Freckles. Hers are too faint. I like the kind that stand right out in a brazen sort of way. Why did I write the letter to the *Call?* Why, because you asked me to, that night in the chem lab at Harkness. My gosh, you little nut, why else would I write it? Didn't you tell me you always thought of me with a sword in my hand avenging injustices?"

"And a blue cape with a red lining," Beany added raptly. "Norbett, do you know what?"

"What?"

"I—I didn't ask you to take me to Miss Hewlitt's—to—to make a sucker out of you. Or—or even to get you out of chem lab. That was—was just an excuse," she admitted shyly.

His laugh was a little choked. "Gosh, Beany, that's what made me go berserk. That was the unkindest cut of all. Because—well, you know I told you once that I never knew anyone with such honest eyes. And I'm not as poor a speller as I let on. I'd say to myself, 'I don't believe her eyes are as blue and as honest and as nice as I thought.' And then I'd ask you something just to see."

"And were they?"

"Uh-huh. Even bluer and honester and nicer than I'd remember."

They looked at each other and laughed—as though the world and this corner here on College were warm and gay.

It even surprised Beany to see people going by, their faces blue and pinched with cold, their necks hunched into pulled-up coat collars. Why, the snow wasn't cold—it was exciting and gladsome and enchanting . . . "Oh, what a beautiful morning! Oh, what a beautiful day!" . . .

Mr. Downey was edged in between the magazine rack

and the big glass window and was painting a sign to lure customers in. It seemed to Beany that he was spelling out, "Beany Malone, it isn't so bad to stick your neck out. Beany Malone, aren't you glad your heart didn't stay locked up— oh, aren't you glad?"

But what the druggist was lettering on his glass window for all the world to read was, "Peppermint Stick Candy Today." And Norbett was saying, "I could buy my girl some peppermint stick candy."

Beany giggled, full of happy plans. "I could make some peppermint-stick ice cream. We had it that first day when I asked you to the party." And suddenly the thought of pink ice cream didn't make her the least bit sick. For suddenly she knew for a certainty that the Malone way, which had seemed wrong these last months, was quite right now.